IT BREAKS ME

BETRAYAL
BOOK TWO

PENELOPE SKY

HARTWICK PUBLISHING

Hartwick Publishing

It Breaks Me

Copyright © 2024 by Penelope Sky

All rights reserved.

No part of this book may be reproduced in any form or by any electronic or mechanical means, including information storage and retrieval systems, without written permission from the author, except for the use of brief quotations in a book review.

CONTENTS

1. Axel — 1
2. Scarlett — 17
3. Axel — 31
4. Scarlett — 45
5. Axel — 65
6. Scarlett — 77
7. Scarlett — 91
8. Axel — 105
9. Scarlett — 115
10. Axel — 137
11. Scarlett — 141
12. Axel — 157
13. Scarlett — 173
14. Axel — 185
15. Scarlett — 195
16. Axel — 225
17. Scarlett — 237
18. Axel — 279
19. Scarlett — 301
20. Axel — 321
21. Scarlett — 339

1

AXEL

SIX MONTHS LATER

I hadn't seen my parents in six months.

They'd blocked my number, so I couldn't text or call, and whenever I showed up to their residence, the guards barred my entry. Trust meetings took place in their absence, their lawyers acting as their puppets. The message was quite clear—I would never speak to them again.

But I knew they would be at the art auction this year, a social event they'd attended every year for the last thirty years, and while it wasn't the best place to provoke them, I needed a chance to say my piece.

I didn't inform anyone that I was attending, because if I did, they were certain not to show up. And sneaking into a hoity-toity party like that was easy. Security only watched the main entrance, but no one hit the main entrance when they snuck into a party anyway.

I walked down the alley and used the back entrance, waiting for one of the workers to step out and carry the trash to the dumpster against the adjacent building. He didn't notice me, so before the door closed and would require his keycard to unlock it, I slipped inside. In my tux with my hair slicked back, I moved down the hall and encountered one of the workers. "Bathroom?"

"Down the hall to the right," he said.

"Thanks." I ignored the directions I didn't need and stepped into the ballroom where the party was being held. Art pieces were on display, from both new and old artists, and champagne and hors d'oeuvres were being served by waiters. A small symphony played music in the corner, clichéd musical entertainment, and everyone there was rich and intent on showing everyone else just how rich they were.

I scanned the crowd and spotted my parents. My mother was in a black gown with sleeves and diamonds in her earlobes, and my father wore a tux identical to mine. They spoke with a couple I didn't recognize. As I stared, I wondered if anyone ever asked them about me, and if they did, how did they react. Did they just ignore the question? Did they really pretend they didn't have a son?

Someone appeared at my side. "You made it."

I kept my eyes on my parents. "The back entrance is more my style these days."

"So I've heard." He cocked a smile.

I hadn't smiled in six months.

Theo took a drink from his glass. "How do you want to play this?"

"Tell them you have a special piece you're only showing a certain clientele. Their egos will diminish all suspicion."

"Alright."

"And then make sure they don't leave until I'm finished."

"Easy enough."

"But no guns."

His eyebrows furrowed as he looked at me. "What if they try to call the police?"

"Then take their phones."

"What if they scream?"

"Then tell them to stop."

"Just showing a gun gets a lot more done—"

"No guns." I stared Theo down.

He stared me down in return. "You know, family reunions aren't really in my job description."

"But I am."

He stared at me before he took another drink. "Ready for this?"

"Yeah. See you in a minute." I headed down the long hallway and into the empty room that we'd already selected. It was far enough away from the party that a commotion would be inaudible. I moved to the other side of the door, so they wouldn't see I was there until they were fully inside and the door was closed.

I waited for several moments, my heart pounding in my chest, a drum against my ribs. The sight of me standing there would be unwelcome, would probably cause a panic, but I was left with no other choice.

The door opened a moment later, and Theo let my parents enter first before he shut the door.

My father looked around the empty room, which only held a table and six chairs. There was no artwork on the walls either, so there was nothing for them to examine. "Where is the painting?" He turned around to face Theo, and he froze when he saw me leaning against the wall. He didn't gasp, but the breath he sucked inside was audible like the wind on a stormy night.

My mother turned next, and she was the one who gave a gasp. "Alexander…"

My father looked at Theo again like he wanted to make a break for it, but when he saw the way Theo leaned against the door with his arms crossed over his chest, he didn't try. He swallowed before he grabbed my mother and tugged her close. "Get behind me, Dorace."

I started to approach them, my hands in my pockets. "I just want to talk."

He continued to back up, keeping my mother behind him, his hands up like I had him at gunpoint.

"Jesus fucking Christ," Theo snapped. "He's not going to hurt you."

My father glanced at him before he started to move away from him too.

Theo rolled his eyes.

I pulled out one of the chairs and took a seat. "I just want to talk. Please."

They stopped against the other wall, nowhere else to go.

Silence ensued, my father's eyes shifting back and forth between Theo and me, unsure who was the bigger threat.

"Let me put it this way," Theo said. "No one is leaving this room until you speak to your son."

The fear in my father's chest wasn't enough to prevent what he said next. "This man is not my son."

Theo moved from the door and raised his voice. "Sit your ass down."

"Theo—"

"Now." He yanked back two chairs and gestured to them.

Both of my parents breathed hard, looking at the chairs awaiting them. They trembled before they obeyed.

"Good." Theo returned to the door and leaned against it again.

My father had his arm around my mother, trying to soothe her shaking limbs. They were so scared, they acted like they were hostages with bombs strapped to their chests. Neither of them looked at me, keeping their eyes on the table.

It pissed me off and made me feel like shit simultaneously. "I've never hurt you, and I'm never going to hurt you."

My dad lifted his gaze to me, and his fear was quickly replaced by rage. "It's taken five surgeries to repair my arm—and it still hurts like a motherfucker. It'll never be the same, and that's because of *you*."

That did make me feel like shit. "I'm sorry that happened, but I had nothing to do with it—"

"Nothing to do with it?" Now my mother piped up when she normally held her silence, probably fully on my father's side now that his arm was permanently injured. "You're the reason your father was targeted. You're the reason he was shot."

"And in case you don't remember, I gave in to his demands to spare your life. Even though you've treated me like shit for five years. Even though you've disowned me completely. And the price I paid for that —" I hadn't seen her in six months, but her face remained burned into my memory. I had pictures of her on my phone, smiling in the bathtub, sleeping beside me in bed, but I never let myself look at them. "Was immense."

"Not more immense than a broken arm," my father snapped.

A painful smirk moved over my lips. "Trust me, I'd take your broken arm any day."

"No respect," he said coldly. "No fucking respect."

"I saved your life, Father. So I'd say I do respect you."

My mother kept her eyes down like she didn't want to look at me.

My father continued to rub her arm.

Empty silence followed.

I wasn't sure what I hoped to accomplish here. Our relationship was more strained than it'd ever been. "I'm really sorry about what happened. Truly, I am."

They said nothing.

"You didn't deserve that." Dante had put the final nail in the coffin, and now there was no hope for reconciliation. I wanted to kill him for that, but I couldn't do a damn thing.

"We didn't deserve to have such a piece-of-shit son either," Father said coldly.

"I really didn't do it. She set me up because I tried to leave her."

Both of them ignored me.

"I'm telling you the truth."

"Even if you are telling the truth," my mother said. "It wouldn't change anything. Your father could have died because you've chosen this lifestyle. That's completely on you. You're a liar. You're a criminal. You're a murderer."

"We tried so hard to have you," Father said. "Endless doctor's visits and procedures…and then we were finally given a miracle. But now I wish we'd just accepted our fate. Our lives would have been far better."

I was a grown man roughened by life, but I'd have to be devoid of all emotion for that not to bother me. It was like a knife in an old wound, except this time, it went a little deeper than before.

I could feel Theo staring at the side of my face. Feel his angry glare burn my cheek.

"If I walk away from this life, can we try to reconcile?" I didn't have much to live for these days. The one thing that gave me meaning had been stripped away, and now I realized how lonely I was.

My father's answer was immediate. "No."

"Never," my mother added.

"If you really are sorry for what happened, you'll take the check and leave us alone," Father said. "Dismiss yourself from the trust and disappear for good."

"Would you also like me to shoot myself in the head?" I said it in a defeated voice because I really believed that my own parents wouldn't even come to my funeral. "Would that make you happy?"

They stayed quiet.

I nodded to Theo.

Theo hesitated before he stepped away from the door to allow them to escape.

My parents hesitated before they moved for the door, like it was some sick trap. They eyed Theo like he was about to pull out a gun and shoot them both. They crept toward the door, sticking to the other wall.

Theo stood there with his hands in the pockets of his slacks.

When my parents finally reached the door, Theo jerked forward just to spook them.

My mother gave a scream, and they ran into the hallway.

Theo shut the door and sighed before he joined me at the table, sitting where my father had sat a moment before.

I sat with my elbows on the table, staring at my hands as one massaged the other, feeling old pains in my knuckles from fights long forgotten.

Theo stared at me.

I kept my eyes down, doing my best to ignore the throbbing pain in my chest.

"I'm sorry, man."

"It's fine," I said immediately. "That's how I expected it to go."

"You wouldn't have bothered if you'd really thought that."

My hands stilled at his observation. After a pause, I continued to soothe the aches.

"Kill Dante. He deserves to die for this."

"He deserves to die for a lot of reasons."

"Then let's do it. Let's put a bullet in that fucker's head and get your girl back."

"She's not my girl anymore." It'd been six months. And in those six months, we hadn't spoken to or seen each other. Dante prohibited me from visiting his property, so all our meetings took place in hotel lobbies or in office buildings. I'd been tempted to text her, but I knew it would just fuck with her head and make it harder.

"He still should be in the ground."

I lifted my chin and pulled my hands back. "I can't."

"Why?"

"You know why."

"You just said she's not your girl anymore."

I swallowed. "I still couldn't do that to her."

"I bet if she knew, she would give you her full permission."

I shook my head slightly. "She'd be angry. Maybe cut him out of her life. But she would never wish her father dead."

Theo watched me.

"I hate my father…but I would never wish that."

Theo leaned back in the chair, his hair slicked back and his tux tight on his shoulders. "You know what I think?" His thick arms crossed over his chest. "I think you're too fucking nice, Axel."

My eyes flicked away.

"And you know what happens to nice guys? They get fucked over."

"Oh, I know."

"We can't kill Dante, but that doesn't mean we can't get revenge."

"When did this become a *we* situation?" I turned back to him. He had his own shit to take care of. His own business ventures that took up every minute of his day.

"The moment I heard your parents say that god-awful shit to you."

"What's your idea?" I'd been too depressed these last six months to care about revenge. I spent most of my free time with my wet bar, watching TV alone while life continued without me. Even when I saw Dante, I felt nothing. The last time I'd felt something was when I'd walked into that restaurant with Cassandra and broke my woman's heart.

"You think Dante will drop you if he finds someone better?"

I gave a painful chuckle. "In a heartbeat. But no one can make him the kind of money I can."

He grinned. "Except me."

My eyes narrowed on his face. "I know we both hate him, but he's not someone to cross. I appreciate your loyalty, but you don't need to get your hands dirty because he fucked me over."

"Yes, I do."

I cocked my head slightly.

"Because you would do it for me."

2

SCARLETT

The SUV pulled up to the plant, and one of the guys opened the back door for me to step out. It was overcast, the pavement wet from the midnight rain, and I felt the tiny pieces of gravel underneath my heels.

I walked forward, and the entourage of men assigned as my security detail followed me from a distance, two of them with automatic rifles and the others with handguns. I opened the door and stepped inside the plant, a production company for biscotti that were packaged and shipped overseas for Americans to enjoy. It was a company my father owned, just to wash his money, a company that beat all its competitors because the prices were so low. But the prices were so low because my father didn't care about being very profitable. It was just for appearances.

I headed downstairs and stepped through the hidden door in the wall then walked into the part of the lab that actually mattered—where our product was manufactured. Instead of blue-collar workers dressed in stained uniforms, we had a sea of white coats and goggles. My father used to get his product from other producers, but they were unable to keep up with his demand, so he ventured into the business himself.

The men looked up when I appeared. They all stood at different parts of the counter, in different phases of the production of our product. They stared at me just the way they stared at my father—like they were terrified.

I walked to the plastic tubs where the product was visible. "Rigo, get the scale. Tom, move the crates. We're going to weigh every single one of these to make sure nothing is missing." I looked at the men in the laboratory, wanting to see their faces after I declared my intention.

They all looked back down and got to work.

My father didn't suspect anyone was stealing, but it was best to give them a reason not to try.

At the end of the day, I returned to my father's estate.

It was about to rain, the gray clouds overhead heavy with condensation. The sound of thunder erupted in the distance just as I stepped inside, surrounded by the warmth of his home. I shed my jacket and left it on the coatrack then moved farther inside his mansion, a place far too big for a terminal bachelor.

I hoped to have a place like this someday.

Ever since I'd assumed more responsibility, I was able to leave my old apartment and get a much nicer place. It was three times the size of my old place, had an underground parking garage for my car, and had a chef's kitchen that had become my playground. Whenever I was home from work, I spent my time cooking, trying new recipes and bringing leftovers to the office for lunch.

I stepped into his office and found him behind his big mahogany desk. "It's all accounted for. No one's skimming off the top."

"Good." He finished reading the email on his laptop before he shut it. "I suspected as much."

"They look scared. I don't think we need to worry about them."

His hands came together on the table. "I like it when people are scared." He gave me a smile, his warmth a contradiction to his cold statement. "You have the paperwork?"

"I just sent it to your email before I walked in."

"Great," he said. "How are you?"

"Fine. You?"

He got comfortable in the leather chair. "I'm really asking, sweetheart."

"Oh." It was such a meaningless exchange of words that I never took the question seriously. "Good," I said. "I've been cooking a lot. I really love my new kitchen. My other place was so small and cramped."

"Invite me over for dinner sometime. I'd love to eat your cooking."

"Sounds like fun," I said. "I'll let you know."

He gave me a smile. "Have you been seeing anyone?"

I gave a slight shake of my head. "Not really. Nothing serious, at least." It was hard to date other men after

Axel. Not because he broke my heart and destroyed my ability to trust, but because my standards were much higher now, and it was impossible to find a suitable replacement. I didn't want to settle for a man who made me come once in a while. Now, I wanted a man who could do it every time, who was serious but not serious about himself. But even if I did find that man, I'd just assume it would end with his infidelity—because a man like that was just too good to be true.

My father didn't ask more questions on the topic. "I have a meeting tomorrow night with a new distributor. I'd like you to come with me. Your opinion means a great deal to me."

"A new distributor?" The last time I'd seen Axel was in that restaurant. My text never got a reply. I had no idea if he even knew I'd spotted him because he didn't care enough to contact me again. Maybe my father had said something, but he'd never told me about it. But I knew Axel no longer came to the estate, and our paths never crossed because he was prohibited from any space I might occupy. When my father didn't invite me to social events, I knew it was because Axel would be there. Maybe he wanted to spare me the pain. Or maybe he just didn't want that asshole to breathe the same air as me.

"Yes, I think I've found a suitable replacement."

Dread formed in my heart—along with a dose of guilt. "Based on the numbers I see, we don't need a replacement." Axel continued to do his job and had even expanded our business to territories that had once been off-limits.

My father stared me down. "I disagree."

"If this is because of me…it's completely unnecessary."

My father's expression didn't change much, but his anger was palpable.

"I can be in the same room with him. It was a long time ago, and I'm over it. I have no doubt we can be professional toward each other, so this separation is also unnecessary." When I'd spotted him with Cassandra, I'd gone home and cried…and cried. I'd worked from home for a week because I couldn't get myself out of bed. My father gave me space and didn't ask any questions about my absence, probably knowing exactly why I needed to stay home. For a solid month, I was dead inside.

And I guess I was still a little dead, just in a different way.

My father continued his stare. "I don't like him."

"He does his job and he does it well, so that's irrelevant."

"Then let me rephrase that. I hate that motherfucker." My father never cursed in my presence, rarely showed his rage, but he opened the lid and released the steam. "I've wanted him gone for a long time, and now I can finally rid myself of that trash."

I absorbed my father's rage and let it dissipate. "I think it's unwise to gamble what we have when we have no idea if this new distributor will be an improvement. And once Axel is gone, we won't be able to get him back." He wasn't as stubborn as my father, but he definitely had his pride. And since he hated my father, I knew he wouldn't be eager to work with him again, not for all the money in the world.

"Trust me, this guy is an improvement."

I felt no allegiance to Axel, not after what he did to me. And I wouldn't want to work with him directly once my father stepped down. That would be shitty. But I saw Axel's work on a daily basis, and I knew he was a great partner to have, not someone to be dumped so carelessly…even though he'd dumped *me* carelessly. "Who is he?"

My father relaxed in his chair, his anger starting to evaporate. "The Skull King."

The restaurant was empty when we walked inside, fully booked out for this meeting. I wasn't sure if my father was responsible for that or the Skull King. I'd heard of the Skull King but never met him. He was the unofficial prime minister of the country, pulling the strings of the puppets in government, taking tariffs on all illegal commodities shipped through the country as payment for his services. He had his hand in other industries too, from what I understood.

His men were positioned throughout the restaurant, standing in the dark corners and sitting at empty tables, all armed.

My father led the way and then reached the table in the center of the room, the Skull King sitting there alone.

He was not what I'd pictured.

He was young, good-looking, muscular. He had dark hair and dark eyes, a beard that traced his hard jawline. He looked a couple years older than me, in his early thirties, very young to have attained this kind of power.

My father greeted him first. "Been a long time." He extended his hand for a shake.

The Skull King rose to his feet and shook my father's hand. He was over six feet, taller than my father. When he greeted my father, it was with a slight smirk on his lips, like this was a great pleasure…or a joke. "It has. You're looking fit, Dante."

My father gave a chuckle. "I do what I can." He turned to me. "Theo, allow me to introduce my daughter, Scarlett."

I moved to him next, refusing to be intimidated by a man hailed as a legend. I extended my hand to shake his. "Lovely to meet you."

He grabbed my hand and gripped it tightly, his dark eyes shifting back and forth between mine as he shook it. Then a smirk moved on to his lips as he pulled away. "You really are beautiful…" The smirk remained, like he knew something I didn't, told a joke and I'd missed the punch line.

"Thank you…"

Theo nodded to the table. "Sit." Before he took a seat, he pulled out the chair for me, something my father would normally do for me.

As I sat down, Theo pushed the chair in then took a seat to my right, across from my father. He crossed one leg, resting his ankle on the opposite knee, and he wore a black long-sleeved shirt with no jacket, even though it was freezing outside. Last night, we'd had a frost, and the frost was already settling in again this evening.

The waiter arrived and brought a bottle of wine for the table before he poured the glasses. We weren't asked what we wanted because Theo seemed to have already made the decision for everyone.

My father took a drink. "Excellent choice." My father turned the bottle to look at the label. "The Pearl, Barsetti Vineyards, 2016. That was a good harvest." He turned the bottle back around.

"Are we here to talk about wine or money?" That knowing smirk was gone, and now Theo was all seriousness. His focus was reserved for my father, and he didn't seem interested in me anymore.

"Very well," my father said. "If we formed a partnership in distribution, not only will you receive your tariffs, but also ten percent of the proceeds from our product movement. And on a weekly basis, that amounts to…" He turned to me since I looked at the numbers all day.

"Twenty million," I answered. "We've also increased production, so we'll have more product in the coming weeks. We'll need additional partners to fulfill these orders. We hope that you have the connections to expand our business."

"Twenty million a week." He paused to mull that over. "That's impressive."

"Thank you," my father said.

"It sounds like your current distributor is doing a fine job, so why do you need me?"

My father paused as he considered his answer. "I know you can do better."

"But changing distributors will be a lengthy process. Is it worth an additional five million?"

"Five million more is five million I don't have," my father said simply.

"And your distributor can't expand further?" Instead of just taking the job, he chose to dig, like he wanted all the specifics before he agreed. It was tedious, but it was smart.

My father took a drink as he considered what to say. "We're personally incompatible."

Theo stared at him for several seconds. "And why are you incompatible when you're making money hand over fist together?"

"Because I don't like him."

"Why?" Theo pressed.

My father struggled to maintain his composure, tired of talking about Axel and wanting to avoid all the specifics. "Because he's a piece of shit. That's why." My father's words had a tone of finality to them, a barrier Theo shouldn't cross.

Theo rested his fingers on the stem of the wineglass, staring at my father across the table with eyes so confident they looked hostile. "I have a lot of shit on my plate, so if you want me to take this on, it's going to be fifteen percent."

My father stilled at the counteroffer. "If you take fifteen percent, then you're going to have to bring in additional business. Otherwise, the partnership doesn't make sense."

"It makes sense if you hate your current distributor enough."

I realized we had played right into his hands. He wanted to know everything about Axel to figure out how much we needed him, and now that he knew, he used it as leverage.

"As for the additional business, I'll see what I can do," Theo said. "The French territory is in a state of limbo right now with Bartholomew out of the game. Word on the street is a new guy is coming to the stage, and he's not to be crossed."

"We have a deal, then?" my father asked.

Theo nodded toward me. "What's her part in this?"

"She works for me," my father said. "And someday, she'll replace me."

"Really?" He turned to look at me, sizing me up like I was an opponent rather than a pretty face. "Scary place for a woman who's the size of a broomstick."

"This broomstick can break your jaw in a single hit," I said automatically.

My father issued a quiet warning. "Scarlett…"

But a slow smile moved on to Theo's face, like he found me charming rather than disrespectful. "It's fine, Dante. She's cute." He grabbed his glass and took a drink. "I might have to take you up on that offer, sweetheart."

"So, we have a deal?" Dad repeated, eager to close the books on Axel and start something new.

"No deal." Theo drained the glass until there was nothing left. "I need to think about it."

My father hid his disappointment as best he could. "I understand."

Theo rose to his feet, ready to dismiss us. He shook my father's hand before he turned to me. When he took my hand, he squeezed it hard again, and that playful smirk reappeared. "Goodnight, Scarlett. I hope we see each other again soon…"

3

AXEL

Theo sat in the armchair and put his feet on the coffee table. "You failed to warn me how fine she was." A cigar was between his fingers, and his elbow was propped on the armrest. He tilted his head back and let the smoke slowly dissipate from his mouth.

I sat in the other armchair across from him, in his living room, the furniture made of wood, the walls made of black marble, the room dark except for the dim lighting from the lamps in the corners. "Because it was never relevant to the story."

"I think it's pretty fucking relevant," he said with a chuckle.

I didn't want to listen to Theo tell me how sexy she was, but I really had no reason to be upset about it. Six months had come and gone. She'd probably been with other people, and I knew I had. She wasn't mine anymore. "How was she?"

Theo gave a shrug. "Didn't say much. Except for when I called her a broomstick and she threatened to break my jaw." He grinned. "She's got some spice to her."

"She does." I missed that spice. But it also told me she was fine, that she was her old self, that she had moved on. I was relieved by that information…but also disappointed. Other women might have been in my bed, but no other woman had been in my heart. With Scarlett, I'd been evicted. "Anything else?"

"No amount of spice is going to keep that pretty head on her shoulders when her father is gone. He is either in denial or doesn't give a shit about his daughter if he thinks this is a good idea."

"I agree," I said. "I think there's another piece we're missing—and so is Scarlett." I worried about her just as much now as I did before. She would walk into a lion's den without anyone to watch her back. No man would take her seriously in negotiations, and it would be a contest to see who could pin her down and fuck her in the ass first. I'd never said that to her because I didn't want to scare her, but now I wished I had.

Theo enjoyed his cigar in silence, in his black jeans and gray t-shirt, his black boots on the wooden table.

"How long are you going to wait?"

He let more smoke escape from his mouth. "Until he comes to me. I want to see how desperate he is."

"Oh, he's fucking desperate."

"You'd think the guy would let the past go and move on."

"No. Once his new partnership is thriving and I'm out of the picture, he'll try to kill me since Scarlett will have no way of knowing. That's why he doesn't let us interact, so she won't know when I'm dead."

He chuckled. "Damn, that man knows how to hold a grudge."

"And so do I."

His butler announced himself by clearing his throat before he approached Theo. "Dante has come to pay you a visit. Shall I invite him inside or send him away?"

Theo looked at me, his grin unmistakable. "I expected the guy to play it cool a little longer."

"I told you he's desperate."

"I wonder if he's brought me gifts." His grin stretched.

"I think I know exactly what he brought you." I put out the cigar in the ashtray and tossed it aside. "I'll listen from in here." The next room over was a spare bedroom, and I left the door wide open like it'd been before. There was a chair on the other side, so I took a seat, and the mirror on the wall gave me a view of the living room.

Theo turned to his butler. "Show him inside."

"Yes, sir."

Theo kept his position, slouched in the armchair with the cigar in his mouth.

A moment later, Dante entered. "I hope you don't mind my dropping by. I was in the neighborhood."

Theo rose from his chair and shook his hand. "Your timing couldn't be better. The girls just left."

Dante moved into the armchair I'd just vacated, and I wondered if he noticed the warmth of the cushions from where my body had been just minutes ago.

I moved closer to improve the line of sight from the mirror now that Dante faced the opposite direction, and I propped my elbow on the armrest and curled my fingers under my chin, ready to listen to the exchange in comfort.

"You got a girl, Dante?" Theo asked.

"No."

"No special lady?"

"No," Dante repeated. "But I have lovers...several of them."

"Your wife die or something?" Theo asked bluntly, already knowing the story but pretending he didn't.

"No. We were just fucking, and Scarlett was a surprise. I raised her on my own."

"Wow...Daddy's little girl."

Dante said nothing to that.

"Probably not my place to say anything, but you've got to be stupid to think she can handle that empire by herself. She seems smart, she's got spice, which I like, but come on, Dante. You're fattening the lamb for the slaughter."

Dante remained quiet.

When Theo didn't get a response, he carried on. "What brings you by?"

"Wanted to know if you've given my offer further thought."

Theo enjoyed his cigar in silence, waiting until it was uncomfortable with tension, giving Dante a taste of his own medicine. "I've been busy, Dante."

"I'm sure," Dante said cordially, acting like a little bitch because he wanted to get rid of me so badly. He'd rather suck up to the Skull King than break bread with me. That was a profound level of hatred. He would definitely try to kill me once he had that chance.

"There's only so much time in the day, and it's hard to decide what to do with the minutes I have left. I could spend them at the whorehouse or with my regulars… or I could spend them with you. It's a tough call."

I smirked and wished I could see Dante's reaction to all this.

"Well, your whores will only make you poorer, and I'll make you richer."

Theo grinned, holding the cigar in his mouth. "Good one, Dante."

Dante tipped his head slightly in an *I thank you* gesture.

"But I need more time to think it over," Theo said. "Feel free to take a cigar for the ride home."

I knew Dante hadn't come here empty-handed. I waited.

Theo waited too, bringing the cigar to his lips for a taste of the leather-flavored smoke.

Dante remained in the chair and didn't reach for the cigar. "Perhaps this will sway you…" He reached inside his coat and pulled out a box.

I fucking knew it.

He moved to the other side of the coffee table and handed Theo the box before he took a seat again.

With the cigar in his mouth, Theo sat forward and popped open the lid.

I couldn't see with the lid open, but I already knew what was inside.

A Skull Ring.

Theo stared for a moment before he pulled out the cigar and set it in the ashtray beside him. A quiet whistle escaped his lips as he regarded it. "I'm not going to ask where you got this."

"And I'd appreciate that."

He pulled the ring out of the box and slipped it onto his middle finger. He angled his hand left and right, letting the light catch the brilliance of the diamond. Appreciation came over his face, intrigued by the stunning perfection of the one-of-a-kind ring. "The other two?"

"They're yours if we have a deal."

Theo continued to stare at the ring, no smile on his face. "It would take you two years to earn what you could sell these for." He lifted his gaze and looked at Dante.

"I thought I would return them to their rightful owner," he said. "And I know, with your connections, you can bring a lot more than five million to the table. Together, I think we could easily double our weekly revenue."

Theo's finger curled into a fist to test the way the ring felt against his knuckle.

Theo was loyal to me, but nevertheless, it was a reasonable temptation. Those rings were a legend, and anyone who killed the Skull King claimed his rings as a trophy. They'd been sold to other buyers since, but Dante had stolen them back. He'd been plotting this for a long time, probably before we formed our partnership.

Theo stared at him. "This offer just got more enticing."

I imagined Dante was smiling. "Ten percent. These rings cover the extra five percent you added."

Theo gave a nod. "You have a deal."

"I have another request." Dante sat up, leaning forward with his arms on his thighs.

Theo smirked. "Don't get too carried away now. I could just kill you and take these."

"Which is why I only brought the one," Dante said coldly. "And I'm the only one who knows where the other two are located."

Theo's smile faded. "What's your stipulation?"

Dante was quiet for a long time, like he was having second thoughts about the request. He was right at the finish line, but something tripped him up. "I want you to marry my daughter."

A rush of adrenaline flooded my blood and fueled my muscles for battle. The edges of my vision blurred with the color red. I could feel the spike in my heart rate, but I could also hear it in the pounding in my ears.

What the fuck did he just say?

Theo's eyes flicked to mine in the mirror just for a nanosecond. He corrected himself instantly, shifting his gaze toward the window like his stare had been a meaningless reaction. He kept his gaze there, probably to look convincing. "Did you just ask me to marry your daughter?" He turned back to Dante, his perplexed reaction completely genuine.

I was about to storm out of there and choke Dante from behind then burn his eyes with a hot cigar. He'd taken Scarlett away from me, and then he offered her to Theo…who didn't even fucking know her.

"Yes," Dante said calmly. "I did."

"And you don't think that sounds crazy?" Theo asked incredulously. "Is this the fifteen hundreds and you're marrying your daughter off to a king for political gain?"

"Yes." Dante said it just as calmly as before. "That's exactly what I'm doing."

Theo continued to look at him like he was crazy.

"You're a king, Theo. Not a king that wears a crown, but a king nonetheless," he said. "I need to know my daughter will be safe when I'm gone, and I know you'll be able to take care of her. You can acquire the business as part of the marriage, so that's another asset under your belt. And then her children will take over once they're of age. It's my legacy—and I want you to safeguard it."

I couldn't believe this bullshit.

"How do you know I'll treat her right?"

"You don't strike me as the wife-beating and lying type."

"I'm not," Theo said. "But I don't know how you would ever know that."

"I have my people. I hear things."

He obviously didn't hear everything because he had no idea what kind of relationship Theo and I had.

"I'm not looking to get married, Dante," Theo said. "Never been interested in that."

"Have you seen my daughter?" Dante asked in disbelief. "You know the blood that runs in her veins. She would give you beautiful children. Maybe you don't want a wife, but you certainly want your legacy to continue."

He treated her like a horse to be bred.

"Dante, even if I agreed to this, what makes you think she would agree to it?" Theo asked. "She doesn't strike me as a woman who would marry a fucking stranger."

"Then don't be a stranger," he said. "Take her out to dinner. Wine and dine her. You're a very handsome man. You should have no problem getting her to say yes."

So, not mixing business and pleasure was a bunch of fucking bullshit.

Theo released a quiet chuckle, finding all of this batshit crazy. "I've been offered a lot of things to forge a deal—including the heads of my enemies—but never this. It's not something I can guarantee because she needs to consent to it."

"She will," he said. "Take her out a couple of times, start a relationship, and when the time comes, I'll make sure she says yes." Dante remained leaning forward. "Do we have a deal, Theo?"

Theo stared at the ring on his hand before he gave a sigh. "Alright."

"Then that ring is yours. You get the second one after our first distribution. And then you get the third when you marry my daughter." Dante got to his feet to shake Theo's hand. "Let's make money together."

Theo stood up and shook his hand. "Yes."

Dante said goodbye then let the butler guide him downstairs and out the front door.

I waited a couple of minutes before I stepped out of the bedroom and approached him.

Theo stood with his arms crossed over his chest, looking at me with a hard expression, like he knew how fucking shitty this was.

I came closer to him and slid my hands into my pockets. "I almost came out here and killed him."

"I was surprised when you didn't."

I stared at the diamond skull on his finger. "I used to believe Dante didn't like me solely because of my past, but now I realize it was always bigger than that. He manipulated Scarlett into dumping Ryan. He manipulated me to stay away from Scarlett. All because he wanted to use her as a bargaining chip."

Theo continued to stare at me with eyes full of pity.

"It's so fucked up."

His hand moved to my arm, and he patted me. "We'll have him by the balls soon, Axel. Just be patient."

4

SCARLETT

I was in the parlor on my laptop when the guards opened the door and Theo stepped inside. The second the door opened, a rush of cold winter air rushed inside and made bumps form on my arms. I was in a long-sleeved V-neck sweater, tucked into my ruffled skirt, so the air was definitely chilly.

My eyes focused on him, his physique stretching the fabric of his long-sleeved shirt nicely. His dark jeans hung low on his hips, and his jawline was clean because he seemed to have shaved that morning. When he spotted me at the table, he took a seat across from me.

I grabbed the top of my laptop and slowly closed it. "Nice to see you again."

He watched me with his hard gaze, a handsome man who probably got tail wherever he went. "Your father and I struck a deal."

My father hadn't mentioned that to me, but I pretended he had. "Looks like I'll be seeing more of you, then." It was the first time I'd seen a man who rivaled Axel in appearance, who had a strong body and thick arms, who had the kind of confidence that could command a room. Theo didn't have beautiful blue eyes and light-colored hair, but he was still hot as fuck.

"I hope so." He continued his stare, able to hold eye contact without flinching.

The stare started to make my skin hot. "I do all the accounting because my father doesn't trust anyone else with the information—"

"Have dinner with me tonight."

I hesitated at the question. "I-I don't mix business with pleasure." The last time I did, I ended up with a broken heart, a heart that was still broken six months later. Axel's betrayal had given me a permanent wound, the kind that scabbed over but never healed. "I think it's best if we just keep our relationship professional—"

"We're having dinner tonight. I'll pick you up at six."

"I'm flattered, but—"

"I asked your father's permission beforehand. He's fine with it."

"You—you did?"

"Yes."

"And he said it was fine?"

He gave a nod.

"Are—are you sure?"

Now he grinned. "He was enthused."

That was the opposite message my father had given me. He said it was important to be professional, always.

Theo's grin remained. "You don't believe me."

"It's just…my father has always said it's unwise to get involved with people from work—"

"Looks like he's made an exception for me." He rose from the table and pushed in the chair. "See you tonight." He turned and headed to the door.

"Wait, didn't you come here to speak to my father?"

He opened the door before he looked at me again. "No."

I watched him go, his tight ass snug in his jeans. After he got into his sports car and drove off, I walked into my father's office where he sat at his desk.

He was on the phone. "Just because the ships are delayed doesn't mean our delivery needs to be delayed. Find another way, Rigo." He hung up then looked at me. "Did you need something, sweetheart?"

"So, Theo was just here…"

"Alright."

"He asked me out…and said you were okay with that?"

"I am okay with that."

I lowered myself into the chair across from him. "I thought we didn't shit where we ate?"

"He's different."

"Uh, why?"

"Because he's the Skull King. He's the biggest player in the game. He's not even a player. He *is* the game."

"And isn't that the very reason I shouldn't get involved with him?"

"There are times to make an exception—and I think Theo is that exception."

I still couldn't believe what I was hearing.

"Do you want to go out with him?"

"I—I don't know…" I'd never considered it an option. I'd just met him a couple nights ago and the conversation had been brief. "He's a handsome guy, but I don't really know him."

"Go out with him and get to know him."

"I just…" The last person I'd dated from this world was Axel. It felt weird to consider going out with someone like that again. "I don't know."

"Go out with him, sweetheart." He gave me an encouraging smile. "See where it goes."

Unlike Axel, Theo knocked on the door instead of letting himself inside like he owned the place. I opened the door to see him standing there with a black jacket over a white tee in dark jeans and boots. He definitely had that tall, dark, and handsome vibe going on.

His eyes dipped down to scan me in my dress. "Very nice."

"You look hot too—I mean nice."

The smirk that moved on to his face was victorious. "Come on, I'm starving."

We left my apartment, and he drove us to the restaurant where I'd met him previously. Except now, it wasn't closed down but open to a thriving crowd. He seemed to have connections to this place, because everyone else waiting for a table was ignored the second he walked inside. He didn't even give a name before he was taken to the same table where we'd sat before. Like last time, he pulled out the chair for me and slid it in to catch me as I sat down. Then he sat across from me and took off his jacket, revealing how strong he looked as his bulkiness stretched the fabric.

The waiter brought the wine without Theo ordering, and then menus were handed to us. I stared at the menu without really seeing what was on it. I was very aware that I was on a date with the Skull King.

The fucking Skull King.

My eyes focused on the menu, trying to find something I could eat that wouldn't splash or make a mess or get stuck in my teeth. I settled on soup and a salad, just because that was the easiest option.

"What are you having?" Theo asked.

"The dinner salad and the soup."

He stared at me, his dark eyes rigid on my face.

"What?"

"I'm taking you out, and you're getting soup and a salad?"

"I just…"

His eyes could command an entire army when he stared like that.

"Um, I'll try the lasagna."

He finally withdrew his stare. "Good."

The waiter returned to take the order, and Theo ordered for both of us before returning the menus. Then he swirled his glass, sniffed it, and took a drink. He licked his lips before he returned the glass to the table.

I took a drink, my quick pulse causing a vibration in my neck that I could feel twitch every second.

His eyes glanced out the window for a moment before they returned to me.

It was quiet. Like he wasn't the best conversationalist.

"Do you own this restaurant?" I asked.

"Yes. So I hope you like it."

"I'm not a picky eater, so no problems there."

"You don't have a refined palate if you're ordering soup and salad."

My eyes narrowed, unsure if that was a joke or an insult.

Then he smiled.

"I was just nervous."

"Nervous about the food?"

"No," I said with a laugh. "On a first date, you don't want to eat something…messy."

"I respect a woman who doesn't give a fuck and just eats what she wants."

"You take women out a lot, then?"

He swirled his wine again. "Occasionally."

"I have to admit, this is weird."

"Why?"

"Because of who you are." I knew his men were parked at the curb and maintaining a perimeter. There were probably men placed at nearby tables, looking like customers while their guns were stowed inside their jackets.

"I like fine dining just like everyone else."

"You just don't…seem like the kind of guy who has dates." Axel didn't have dates. It seemed like he just had fuck buddies…and I was one of them. I imagined he'd ditched Cassandra a long time ago.

He gave a slight shrug. "I don't usually."

"Then why did you ask me out?"

He looked into his glass before he took a drink, a long pause to consider how he might respond. "You're not bad to look at."

I released a chuckle. "Not bad to look at, huh? Well, thank you. You're definitely not bad to look at either."

A handsome smile moved over his lips, playfulness in his eyes.

Silence ensued. I gave him the chance to speak because I felt like I was the one doing all the talking, but nothing was forthcoming. Axel wasn't the most talkative guy either, but conversation always flowed naturally with him.

I wasn't sure why I kept comparing Theo to Axel. I never did that on my other dates. Maybe it was because they were both from the underworld? Or maybe it was because Theo was the first man I was deeply attracted to.

Guess I had a type—the bad boy.

He swirled his glass and took another drink. "I'm not good at this sort of thing."

"Having a conversation?"

"A conversation without a purpose. One that has no direction or agenda. I either tell people what to do, or…I tell other people what to do."

"I get that," I said. "Sometimes I wonder if my father suffers the same affliction."

"Really? He seems chatty to me."

"Romantically. He hasn't had a relationship in a very long time."

"He's young. Still has time."

"I've encouraged him, but he doesn't seem interested."

"It's hard to open your heart to someone when there's an endless line of warm beds." He took another drink, and that was when the basket of bread was delivered. Quiet conversations happened around us. Utensils scraped against plates as people cut into their meals.

"So, you cook?"

"Yes. How did you know that?"

He hesitated as he looked at me, one arm resting on the tablecloth. "Your father mentioned it."

"I recently got a new place that has a bigger kitchen, so I've done a lot of cooking. It's a major time investment and the dishes are a pain in the ass, but there's nothing like a home-cooked meal. Now that you've taken me to your restaurant, I'll have to take you to mine."

"You want to see me again?"

"Maybe," I said noncommittally. "When we get back to my apartment, I can make us dessert."

He stilled as he stared at me, his dark eyes locked on mine with a grip that wouldn't release.

I wasn't sure if I wanted to get serious with someone who was such a big player in the game. That seemed like a complicated relationship. When Axel and I had gotten together, we'd tried to keep it uncomplicated… but that wasn't possible. But it'd been a long while since I'd had a good lay, and Theo looked like just the type.

He took another drink.

I expected some kind of reaction, but he didn't give it.

Another bout of silence stretched, this one longer than the previous one. It lasted until our dinner was brought to us. He'd ordered the Florentine steak with veggies, and I had my lasagna.

We ate in silence.

"Are you looking for anything serious?" he asked out of nowhere.

I finished the bite I'd taken, thinking about the loaded question he'd just asked. "Not right now. I got out of a serious relationship six months ago, and…I haven't been that motivated to get into another one."

He chewed his bite as he stared at me, like he wanted me to go on.

But I had nothing else to say about Axel.

When Theo finished his food, he spoke. "How long were you together?"

"Like a month or two."

"And you consider that to be a serious relationship?"

"I know how that must sound, but it was an intense relationship."

"And it ended badly?" he asked.

I didn't want to sound bitter and angry on our first date, so I preferred not to go into it. "Oh yeah."

He continued to stare, like he wanted more.

"But that's how it goes sometimes." How people ended up married and happy was a fucking mystery to me. Axel and I had seemed like the real deal, and everything he'd said seemed genuine, but then he'd flipped on me so hard that the earth tilted.

"Are you over him?"

I released a laugh. "I'm definitely over that asshole." I sliced my fork into the lasagna and took another bite.

"Because it's fine if you aren't."

"I'm over him," I repeated. "But he fucked me up pretty bad. I don't think I'll ever get over that part."

He watched me, no longer interested in his dinner, only me.

"Some people can look you in the eye and lie straight to your face without skipping a beat. It's hard to see someone's true colors until it's too late, until they already have a hold on your heart and not just your bed. All the things he said and did…made me feel like I actually mattered to him. But then he found someone else and didn't even have the balls to tell me."

"I'm sorry."

I kept my eyes on my lasagna, slicing my fork through the layers. "Like I said, I'm over him. Just not interested in a relationship right now."

"Then why are you here?"

"Come on. Why do you think?" I took a drink of my wine. "Look at you."

This time, he didn't smile.

"Wasn't going to pass up the opportunity."

We entered my apartment, and he took a quick scan. "Nice place."

"That's nice of you to say." He was richer than my father, so his place in Florence was probably a palace, and he probably had a beautiful apartment in Paris and a yacht parked in the harbor at Positano. I walked into the kitchen. "How about pistachio cannoli?"

He followed me into the kitchen and leaned against the island. "You can make that?"

"I can make anything." I moved to the fridge and pulled out the bowl of cream. "I made the pistachio cream this morning. All I need are the shells." I pulled out all the ingredients and got to work.

He watched me, arms crossed over his chest, and he didn't offer to help.

"Take a seat." I gestured to the dining table. "You want some wine?"

He moved to a seat and he sank in the chair, his thick arms resting on the table. "Sure."

I uncorked a bottle and poured him a glass before I got back to work.

In silence, he watched me, his elbow on the table with his fingers pressed against his lips.

I put the shells in the oven to bake before I carried the bowl to him. "Try it." I slid my finger through the cream then held it up for him.

He stared at me before he leaned forward and sucked the cream off my finger, his eyes on me the entire time.

I dropped not-so-subtle hints that I wanted to spend the night with him, but I wouldn't be the first one to make a move. If he wanted me, he had to take me. That was how I liked it. "What do you think?"

He swallowed as his eyes remained locked on me. "Damn."

I smiled then returned the bowl to the counter. I could feel his gaze on my back, feel it on my ass. Thankfully, the shells only took a few minutes because they were so thin, so I pulled them out of the oven, let them cool, and then filled them with the cream. "Here you go." I put it on a little plate and placed it in front of him before I sat beside him, dragging my finger through the cream before I sucked it off. "Damn, that is good."

He picked up the cannoli and took one big bite before he set it back on the plate. He chewed slowly, his eyes on me as he enjoyed it. A spot of cream was in the corner of his mouth, so he swiped it with his thumb before he licked it off. He didn't finish his, like that was the only bite he would allow himself to have.

I ate all of mine, every single bite, leaving a pile of crumbs on my plate.

He stared at me, his fingers rubbing across his jawline even though he'd shaved his beard. His dark eyes were impossible to read, so rigid and hard, they guarded all his thoughts. He knew all he had to do was lean in and kiss me and we would end up in the bedroom, but he remained in place.

I grabbed the plates and carried them to the sink. "Thank you for dinner."

He was quiet.

I turned around and leaned against the counter.

He remained in his chair, staring at me.

My impatience got the best of me. "I basically told you I want to fuck you, and you still haven't kissed me."

An instantaneous smile pulled at his lips, and the grin reached his eyes. He looked at me the way he had when we first met, affection in his gaze. "There's that spice."

"Where's yours?"

With a grin still on his face, he came to me, stopping just inches away.

I stared at him, watched him glance down at my lips before he looked at me again.

Then he closed his eyes and gave a sigh. "I should go."

"Sorry?" I was so shocked by what he'd said that I couldn't stop myself from blurting that out.

"I've got somewhere to be." His eyes were down for several seconds before he looked at me again. "Trust me…I wish I could stay." He stepped away and walked through my living room. "Really, I do."

I was so blinded by his withdrawal it took me several seconds to process what had just happened. Never in all my life had I been rejected like that. I'd offered him a night of passion, no strings attached…*and he had somewhere to be*. But I was too proud to question him or argue about it. His loss.

I met him by the door. "Well, thank you for dinner."

"Thanks for the cannoli." He didn't hug me or kiss me on the cheek…nothing. He walked out and turned down the hallway.

I listened until his footsteps were gone before I shut the door.

I stood in my empty apartment and digested what had just happened, tried to figure out where I went wrong. Did I talk about Axel too much? Did I have a marinara stain in the corner of my mouth the entire time and didn't notice? Or was he just not that attracted to me? Maybe that was it…

5

AXEL

I need to speak with you.

I was on the couch in my bedroom when Dante's message appeared on my phone.

Half an hour. Our usual spot.

I knew the moment had arrived. At least he had the balls to fire me to my face. I expected him to do it over the phone or with a short text message. Or maybe he just intended to shoot me dead. Two birds, one stone. *See you soon.*

I left with my guys, Russell included. Dante and I usually met in private, one or two guys around at the most, but this time, I brought a small army. We arrived at one of Dante's buildings, a property he owned but did nothing with. It was full of old furniture that had collected decades of dust. It served solely as a meeting spot, a private location his daughter probably didn't even know about.

His car was parked outside, so I knew he was already there. I approached the doors with my twelve guys, and the guards at the door immediately narrowed their eyes at my approach. Their hands reached for their guns, but they didn't draw.

It was twelve versus two—so they didn't do shit.

I clapped one on the shoulder. "We come in peace, man." I led the way, taking the stairs instead of the elevator since there were so many of us. Dante's arrogance would be his downfall one day. In a community so small, it was stupid not to be prepared for the chance I found out about his back-alley deal with Theo. The only reason he would survive this meeting was because I cared for Scarlett too much to hurt her.

I entered the double doors, and the guards immediately backed up at the sight of us, having no warning from the men below.

Dante sat in the armchair, his legs crossed, his hands in his lap. He had a subtle reaction to his face, a slight shock that I'd brought so many men with me, but he quickly covered it. "Didn't realize this was a party."

"We just finished a job." I dropped into the armchair across from him. "And since you have your men, I thought I would bring mine." My arms plopped down on the armrests, and I crossed my legs, one ankle resting on the opposite knee. This was the beginning of great things, and I could barely keep my smile in check. Dante was about to royally fuck himself over, and he had no idea.

He stared at me, his eyes hard and serious.

I stared back, holding his gaze as I waited for him to get on with it.

But he remained silent.

"What's the purpose of this impromptu meeting? I'm a busy man, Dante."

He was quiet a moment longer, like his plan was foiled by the guns I'd brought and he was desperately trying to think of another way to finish the job. His fingers moved across his jawline as he felt the stubble on his face. "I think it's time we go our separate ways."

"We've just hit our highest month, Dante."

He released a quiet breath, his eyelids dropping slightly. "You know it's not about the money."

"I've had no contact with your daughter."

"But the damage is done. You hurt her—"

"That's fucking rich."

"She never would have been hurt if you'd listened to my warning." His eyes sharpened with their coldness. "You disrespected me when you crossed that line. I have no desire to work with trash when my business is made of gold. We both know this was going to end."

"When the new regulations kicked in, your business took a nose dive, and I pulled that plane back to cruising altitude. I saved your ass, and you fucking know it. This is a piss-poor way of repaying my kindness."

Dante stared at me.

"Don't cross me, Dante."

His eyes narrowed slightly in provocation.

"We resume our business. And I get your daughter."

His eyebrows lifted, and then a smile moved into his lips. "I've already secured a new partner for distribution. And even if I allowed you to see my daughter, she wouldn't want you. She despises you—almost as much as I do."

"If I tell her what you did, she'll believe me."

"Then by all means," he said. "Enlighten her." He didn't have to issue the threat because it was heavy in the air. "How's your father's arm? I heard about all the surgeries…what a shame."

I showed my greatest act of restraint by keeping my hand away from my gun. My eyes remained on him, wishing I had the privilege of taking the light out of his eyes. "My parents and I were probably never going to reconcile, but now we have no chance…because of you."

"Because of you," he said. "I made my wishes for Scarlett very clear—"

"I told you how I felt about her. That I actually cared about her—"

He exploded out of nowhere, leaning forward in his chair like he was about to launch himself at me. "You aren't good enough for her." The vein popped in his temple, and his words echoed in the nearly empty room. "You're fucking trash. Trash on the bottom of my goddamn loafer. Fucking garbage. Do you understand me?"

I listened to his screams without flinching.

He got to his feet. "We're done here." He buttoned the front of his jacket, his voice normal again but his face still tinted red in rage. "Our business has concluded. You will be paid for your contributions up until today, until this hour. Visit any of my properties or approach me, and I'll blind you with my bullets. Come near my daughter—and I'll do the same to your father."

I spoke in a calm voice. "You'll regret this, Dante."

"I've never regretted anything in my life."

"Well, that's about to change."

He stared at me.

I stared back.

"Should have taken the deal."

He walked up to me, his hands sliding into the pockets of his slacks. He stopped just inches from me, close enough that we could knife each other. "Watch your back, Axel. I'm coming for you."

I entered the bar through the front entrance. The private room was in the back, so I walked through the crowd of people trying to get a drink and headed into the rear. There was a single round table there, away from the music and the conversation.

Theo was already there, a cigar in one hand and a drink in the other.

I took a seat, seeing the glass of scotch Theo had ordered for me. "You know me so well." I took a drink then grabbed a cigar from the tray before I lit up. This one had a hint of cocoa. I let the smoke soak into my tongue and felt the hit of the nicotine almost instantly. "He fired me last night."

Theo was slouched in the chair, relaxed. "How'd that go?"

"It was obvious he planned to kill me then and there."

"You brought your guys?"

"He was outgunned. He had no choice but to let me go," I said. "That means you guys have broken ground on your new business venture."

He nodded. "I just started moving his product. I've taken it to a few other territories, and once I claim the French territory, our profits will be far greater than yours. I have to say…his product is of great quality. I think he should charge more for it."

"I've made the same suggestion."

"Compared to the other shit on the street, it's golden."

"His logic is to be the best and have the best price."

"Maybe if you're selling shit at the outlets," he snapped. "People will respect your product more if you command a respectable price." He put the cigar back into his mouth. "Once I'm more involved with his business, I'll take it from the inside. It'll be ours to do with what we wish—and I'll charge whatever the fuck I want."

I raised my glass before I took a drink. "I can't wait to see his fucking face." Now that this transition had taken place, I couldn't afford to be seen in Theo's company. Otherwise, Dante would be tipped off, so we had to sneak around like clandestine lovers. We sat there and enjoyed our drinks and cigars like kids enjoyed candy on Halloween. "So…how'd it go?" I could barely bring myself to ask the question. The details would make me sick, but my imagination was about to kill me.

Theo looked at me across the table. "You really want to know?"

"Yes…and no."

"Nothing physical happened."

I did my best not to care, but my breath betrayed me when I breathed a sigh of relief. "Did she…like you?"

He stared at me before he took a drink. "I don't think so."

"So, she didn't make a move?"

His answer was immediate. "No."

Theo was one of the best-looking guys I'd seen, apart from myself, and I was afraid one look at him would send her into a whirlwind. Imagining her with any guy made me uncomfortable, but one who could compete with me was a different situation. "And you didn't either?"

"Like I said—nothing happened." He popped the cigar back into his mouth.

"So…was it a boring date?"

"I guess you could say that. I didn't want to be there, and she seemed caught off guard that I asked her out."

"What did you guys talk about?"

He gave a shrug. "Not much. But you did come up…"

My heart gave a painful squeeze. "I'm guessing good things weren't said."

He let smoke float out of his mouth. "No."

I hated Dante more than I ever had. "Fuck."

"She says she's over you…but not over what happened."

"You asked her that?"

"I asked if she was looking for a serious relationship, and she said she wasn't ready after her ex burned her so bad."

"Motherfucker."

"Why don't you just relocate your parents and tell her the truth?"

I gave him an incredulous look. "I can't get my parents in the same room with me, but you think I can convince them to leave their home and go into hiding for who knows how long? Yes, I'm sure they'll jump right on that."

"Sorry, you're right."

"He's got me by the balls, and he fucking knows it."

"But what if I told her?"

My eyes moved back to him.

"You wouldn't be breaking any rules."

"Once he realizes we know each other, he'll figure it out and kill my parents anyway."

"That brings us back to the most obvious solution here," Theo said. "We shank that motherfucker—"

"No."

"She'd be better off."

"Trust me, she wouldn't."

Theo crossed his arms over his chest with the cigar in the corner of his mouth. "You always do everything the hard way."

6

SCARLETT

My father sat across from me in the office as he worked on his tablet.

His assistant walked inside and tapped him on the shoulder. "Theo is here to see you, Dante."

"Great." He kept his eyes on the tablet. "Tell him I'll be there shortly."

She walked out.

My father emailed me a set of documents. "I'll be gone for the rest of the day. Theo and I are meeting our new partners. Once we get everything in order, things should move smoothly."

"So…does Axel know?"

"I dismissed him a week ago."

I shouldn't care whatsoever. He'd been out of my life for months, but now we'd officially severed all ties. A part of me wondered if he'd been blindsided by my father's decision…if he was angry. "He was fine with it?"

My father raised his chin and looked at me. "What else would he be?"

"I—I don't know," I said. "He did a good job."

"Well, Theo will do a better one. Axel has plenty of other business ventures to keep him busy, Scarlett. There's no hard feelings."

"I know things weren't going well for us before Axel helped us—"

"It's done, Scarlett." He didn't raise his voice, but his tone suddenly turned sharp as a knife. He stared at me like he might start to twist that blade and heighten the tension between us.

I saw the warning in his eyes, the potent irritation. "You don't need to hate him on my behalf—"

"I hate him for my own reasons, sweetheart. I'm glad our business relationship has concluded. Neither one of us will need to hear or see that bastard again."

I felt that same urge again, the urge to defend him, when it was unwarranted. Axel didn't deserve my defense, didn't deserve my empathy. Nothing. He'd talked about us having kids together like we would be together forever, but less than a week later, he was fucking someone else.

I shouldn't give a shit…but I did.

"Hello, beautiful."

I looked up when I heard the deep voice, knowing exactly who it belonged to. Theo stood in front of the table, wearing a black leather jacket that was dotted with waterdrops. The weather outside was a downpour. It started last night and was still going strong, flooding most of the streets and staining all the windows with streaks like the glass door of a shower. "Hey, handsome." I flirted back even though it was disingenuous. I'd made a move on him—a lot of moves—and he didn't take the bait.

He sat across from me, espresso eyes regarding me. "What are you doing tonight?"

"Falling asleep to the sound of the rain."

"You like this weather?"

"I prefer summer, but I guess I don't mind it."

"I love it."

"I figured. That's what all men say."

"You want to get dinner?"

"Why?"

He stilled at my question, his sharp eyes focusing. "Eat. Talk. That sort of thing…"

"And then you fuck afterward," I said. "But you don't seem interested in that."

A smirk spread across his face, despite his attempt to force it back. "Believe me, I *am* interested in that."

"Uh-huh."

"Why would I lie?"

"Why would you turn down a woman who asked you to fuck her?"

"You didn't ask me to fuck you—"

"Maybe not in those exact words," I snapped. "But now I am using those exact words. Do you want to come to my place right now and fuck me? You're cordially invited."

The smirk returned, and he turned to look out the window.

"That's what I thought."

"Just think we're rushing into it—"

"There's something you aren't telling me." I closed the laptop so it was easier to stare at him across the table. "I admit I'm not the supermodel-double-zero-with-big-ass-fake-tits type, but I've got an ass you can sink your teeth into and I fuck as hard as I get fucked, so no straight man is going to say no to that." My arms moved to the table. "So…what is it?"

"If this were reversed, you would be an asshole."

"But it's not reversed. I told you exactly what I'm interested in. No relationship. Just a good fuck or two. But you asked me out anyway. I think *you're* the asshole."

He smirked. "Fuck, you're killing me."

"How am I killing you?"

"That spice, man…"

"If you like it so much, why won't you take me up on my offer?"

His eyes moved back to the window, which was being pelted with rain.

"You're married?"

"No."

"You're gay?"

He laughed. "Nope."

"Girlfriend?"

"No."

"Then what is the problem?"

He continued to stare outside, watching the rain streak down to the ground. "I think you're still hung up on your ex." He turned back to look at me. "And I don't want to mess with that."

"I'm not hung up on him," I said. "And even if I were, what does it matter?"

"It just does." He stared at me, his elbow propped on the table, his fingers against his chin. "How about you make me dinner tonight?"

"I only make dinner for a man if he makes me come afterward."

"Fuck." He dropped his chin and gave a sigh. "You're something else, you know that? Now I get it."

"Get what?"

A knowing smile moved across his lips. "Nothing."

"If we aren't going to fuck, I need to get back to work." I opened the laptop again.

"If you were over him, you wouldn't be so averse to a relationship."

My eyes lifted back to his. "Then why don't you help me get over him?"

He didn't smile this time. "I'm serious."

"Theo, why do you care?" We'd met each other barely two weeks ago, had no foundation for anything more meaningful than physical attraction. He was the Skull King, for fuck's sake. Why did he care about my emotional availability?

He looked away again to stare at the rain. His heavy body leaned to one side in the chair, and it was so quiet in the house that the rain was audible against all the windows. Headlights appeared for a brief moment as someone else pulled onto the grounds, probably my father since he'd had a meeting at the Four Seasons for lunch. But Theo continued to stare, the silence trickling by. "I just do."

I had to check the numbers several times, because the total had to be incorrect. But I pulled the numbers again from all the books and entered them into a brand-new spreadsheet just to have a fresh start.

But the numbers were the same.

My father walked into the office, dressed in his gym clothes with sweat stains around his neck and underneath his arms. He seemed to have gotten a late start that morning and hit the gym later than he normally did. I wasn't sure what had kept him up so late last night, but I didn't ask in case I intruded on something private.

"Dad, I checked these numbers like fifty times, and I think they're right."

"Good or bad?"

"Good…definitely good." I printed out the sheet and handed it to him.

He dropped into the armchair and looked through the columns.

"We're making ten times what we were before."

When he lifted his head to look at me, he wore a wide grin. "I told you Theo was better." He tapped his fingers against the paper before he returned it to the desk. "The man gets it done. No one dares oppose him because they're scared he'll snap their neck."

I didn't get that impression from Theo. He wouldn't even hook up with me because he thought I was still hung up on Axel…when I wasn't. Why would I still have feelings for someone who'd treated me like that? I had far too much self-respect. "He seems harmless to me."

"Because he's a gentleman," Dad said. "And that's why I like him." He rose from the chair and headed to the doorway. "I'm going to shower. We should have dinner to celebrate."

"Sure, Dad."

"You can pick the place."

"How are things going with Theo?" my father asked, eating a salad as usual.

"Um, I don't know. It's not really going…"

"Why not?" he asked, pausing his meal to focus on me.

I couldn't tell my father all the details. That would just be awkward. "He's very reserved."

"He's just a quiet guy, sweetheart. Men like that don't talk much."

"And he's really stiff."

"Again, that just comes with the territory."

Axel came from the same world, and he'd never been stiff. He was always forward and direct, easy to talk to, serious at the right time, and unserious at the right time. With Theo, it felt as if I was on a date with a stone statue.

"Give him a chance."

"Why do you like him so much?"

He immediately looked down at his food as his fork pushed things around. "He's an admirable man. Has accomplished more than I have, and he's at least a decade younger. He's good-looking."

He was definitely good-looking...

"If you don't like him, it's fine. But I think you're missing an opportunity here."

Maybe I was being too callous toward Theo. Instead of having things my way, maybe I needed to take things slow like Theo suggested. I already viewed the situation as a pit stop, and maybe that was offensive to him. "I'll give him another shot."

My dad immediately perked up. "I think that's a great idea, sweetheart."

I was on the couch in front of the TV, the rain still tapping endlessly against the windows. Sometimes there was a gust of wind, and that made the sound so intense I couldn't hear the TV for a few seconds. I missed the summer season, the longer hours of daylight, the warmth that stretched late into the evenings. But I knew I wouldn't mind winter if I could share it with a man who kept me warm, who made the evenings cozy rather than lonely. When those thoughts hit me, I thought of Axel…and I didn't know why.

Maybe it was because I didn't get any closure. I never actually confronted him about what happened. I took the high road instead and ignored him, but when he didn't even notice that I'd ghosted him, that seemed to hurt more.

If someone hated you, at least they felt *something* toward you.

But with Axel, it was like he didn't feel anything at all.

Ever since my father had let him go, he'd been on my mind. I wondered how he'd taken the news, if he was upset about the dissolved partnership or if he was relieved to be free of my father.

Before I knew it, my phone was in my hand, and I was typing. *My father told me what happened…just wanted to know if you're okay.* I stared at the message without sending it. I deleted it and put the phone away. But then I grabbed my phone and typed the message again. *My father told me what happened. Just wanted to know if you're okay?* I stared at the screen as I tried to decide whether I should send it. I still had his message thread because I'd never deleted it. The last few messages were from the last fight we'd had, but everything above that was eggplant emojis, heart emojis, pictures of his naked chest and his fat dick…good memories. A rush of sadness filled me, so I deleted the message and put my phone aside.

Maybe Theo was right. Maybe I wasn't totally over him.

7

SCARLETT

The vehicle pulled up to the curb outside the restaurant, the very restaurant where Theo and I had had our first date, the restaurant where I'd met him for the first time. When we stepped up to the door, the place was quiet, shut down for the evening.

I wasn't sure how he stayed in business when he shut down the restaurant whenever he felt like it.

We walked inside, his men positioned at empty tables and in corners, drinking coffee to warm their bellies. Now that Theo and my father had a strong business relationship, I wasn't sure why the armed men were necessary, but my father didn't appear concerned.

I arrived at the table first. "Hello, Theo." I gave him a smile and a knowing look.

"Hello, beautiful." He didn't hug me or kiss me on the cheek. Instead, he pulled out my chair for me.

This man was the biggest prude who ever lived. I took a seat.

My father greeted him next, the two of them shaking hands and exchanging pleasantries. Then we were all seated, wine and coffee served, along with appetizers no one would eat.

"You shouldn't shut down this restaurant so often," I said. "The food is too good."

"We close early on Sundays," he said. "The guys deserve a quiet night."

"Very kind of you," Dad said before he took a drink of his coffee. "So, business has been exceptional. I want to say you exceeded my expectations, but I knew you were capable of profound greatness."

Theo crossed his arms over his chest, and on his left hand was one of the skull rings I'd stolen.

I stared at it, a sliver of guilt rushing through me, because if I hadn't stolen that ring, Axel might still have his job. My eyes flicked back to Theo, wearing a thin, long-sleeved sweater over his mountain of muscles.

"It's what I do," Theo said humbly. "I like money."

"I'll drink to that." My father raised his wineglass and tapped it against Theo's.

I didn't partake in the toast.

Theo drank from his wineglass then shifted his gaze to me.

I stared back but had nothing to say.

My father started to talk specifics about the distribution process and then inquired about the status of the French territory. The men talked back and forth, and I quickly disassociated from the conversation out of boredom. My eyes drifted away, looking across the tables and the men sitting there, and that was when I noticed something out of place.

A man sat with his back to us. Dirty-blond hair. Thick arms. A gray t-shirt despite the fact it was freezing outside and we'd had nonstop rain all week long. Heat suddenly flushed through me, remembering the warmth of his skin underneath the covers, the way he made me sweat when he was on top of me.

But then that warmth was replaced by a warning in my heart. "Dad?"

Theo said something that made him laugh, so he didn't seem to hear me, his eyes reserved for Theo.

"Dad?" I said it a little louder, glancing at all the armed men around us, realizing they weren't there to protect us…just Theo.

He finally turned away from Theo. "Yes, sweetheart?"

My eyes glanced at Theo for a second before I looked at my father again. "I need to speak to you in private."

My father's eyebrows furrowed, but he didn't say anything.

"Let's talk outside. It'll only take a minute."

My father probably found the request annoying, but I'd never done anything like this in my life, so he seemed to give me the benefit of the doubt. He rose to his feet. "We'll return shortly—"

"Sit."

I hadn't risen out of my chair yet, but I went cold at Theo's tone.

My father picked up on it too because he went rigid.

"Now."

My father continued to stare at him before his eyes shifted to me.

"Perhaps I was wrong about your daughter, Dante," Theo said. "She's much more observant than you are. Now sit your ass down before I snap your neck and you crumble into dust."

Oh shit.

My father stilled, his hard eyes on Theo, and then slowly, he returned to his seat.

My heart raced like it never had before. I was chilly moments ago, and now sweat coated my palms. I was unarmed, and so was my father. His men were outside, probably in the car and unaware of the takeover happening right inside.

There was a staredown between the two of them. Theo was relaxed in his chair, eyeing my father across the table.

If my father was afraid, he didn't show it. "Whatever is about to happen," my father spoke with a calm and strong voice, eyeing Theo with a confident gaze. "It doesn't concern my daughter, so please let her leave."

My heart clenched at my father's plea, caring about me and not himself.

A cocky smile moved across Theo's mouth. "Actually, it does concern her, so she stays put."

My father swallowed. "Theo—"

"No one will hurt her, Dante," Theo said quietly. "The only person you should be concerned about right now is yourself."

My father stared him down, powerless in that restaurant, his arm twisted behind his back by Theo's betrayal.

Theo turned slightly over his shoulder. "Where's the man of the hour?"

That was when the man stood up, finished the rest of his wine, and then turned around. Exactly as I remembered, with thick stubble around his jawline, Axel walked toward us in dark jeans and boots, his eyes reserved for my father and not for me, rage in his eyes and mirth on his lips. "It's been a hot minute, hasn't it, Dante?" He dropped into the chair directly across from my father, which was between Theo and me.

The second he was close to me, I inhaled a quick breath, provoked by his proximity but also scared of it. I tried to focus on Theo, but my eyes wanted to stare at the man I hadn't seen in six months. My eyes flicked back to him, his hard jawline, his gorgeous eyes, his lips…his lips that I'd kissed more times than I could count.

Axel relaxed in the chair and stared down my father across the table, a subtle smile on his lips, victory in his eyes.

My father stared back, the vein starting to pop at his temple.

Axel crossed his arms over his chest. "Looks like you met my brother Theo. Small world, huh?"

Brother?

My father remained still as a statue, his face tinted red with anger and the veins along his neck pulsing. But he didn't react. His breaths didn't quicken like mine did.

Axel turned to Theo. "Should you tell him, or should I?"

"That's a tough one." Theo reached into his pocket and pulled out a coin. "Let's flip for it."

"Good idea."

Theo flipped the coin into the air. "Heads." He caught the coin and presented it to Axel. "Looks like I'll be doing the honors."

"Lucky bastard."

Theo looked at my father. "I've doubled the salary of all your men, so they've chosen to work for me. I've officially acquired your business, which Axel and I will run without you. Your product also belongs to me, and we were nice enough to purchase the factory from you instead of just seizing it."

Jesus.

My father said nothing.

"It was my suggestion to shoot you in the head," Theo said. "Because that's what you deserve after all the shit you pulled—"

"Please…" It was the first time I spoke, so scared my hands started to shake in my lap. I kept a straight face and bottled my tears, because my father would want me to be strong, not weak and afraid.

Both Theo and Axel looked at me.

It was the first time Axel actually looked at me, and his stare was soft and gentle…the way it used to be.

Theo looked at my father and continued. "But Axel has mercifully chosen to spare your life. I think a sign of gratitude is in order."

My father didn't say a word.

Axel stared him down and waited for him to comply.

But my father would rather die.

A long silence ensued, a very heavy one.

Theo looked at Axel. "Shoot this motherfucker—"

"You're officially retired, Dante. Enjoy your billions on your yacht. Find a good woman. Spend time with your daughter." Axel stared with his arms still crossed. "Enjoy your life. If you choose to retaliate, I'll choose to kill you." He spoke with a calm voice, but it had a hard edge to it. "You're dismissed."

My father didn't rise from the chair. "You planned this from the beginning."

"No, *you* planned this from the beginning," Axel said. "I knew the moment I saw Scarlett steal that skull ring."

A rush of humiliation swept through me, realizing Axel had known what I'd done before we'd even gotten together.

Axel continued. "Maybe I would have bowed out gracefully and moved on if you hadn't fucked me over in other ways. But you did fuck me over—hard."

I glanced to my father, unsure what other crimes he'd committed.

"Now it's time to take the trash out," Axel said. "And leave it behind a dumpster where it belongs."

My father was so angry, but he didn't say a word. His face was stretched tight, the cords in his neck straining so hard they looked like they might pop. The red flush to his face was the same color as when he'd drunk too much at a party, but his eyes had a vicious bite, like a rabid dog.

I knew the conversation was over.

Axel grabbed my wineglass and lifted it to Theo. "To new beginnings."

Theo did the same. "To new beginnings."

My father rose to his feet slowly, his eyes glued to Axel's face.

I rose to my feet as well, assuming we were about to depart the most hostile conversation of my life.

My father reached for the inside of his jacket to grab his phone, but I knew that wasn't his true aim.

I knew his anger was insurmountable. The rage boiled his blood and charred his logic. He was about to do something impulsive right now, something that would get him shot between the eyes. So I moved my hand to his arm and squeezed it.

My father paused before his eyes shifted to me.

"Let's go home, Dad." I continued my squeeze, needing him to remember that while his business meant everything to him, he meant everything to me. His choice would only end one way, and the satisfaction would only last a heartbeat. His last one.

He took a slow breath before he made the right decision and reached for his phone.

When we made it home, most of the men were gone, now on Theo's payroll. Only a few remained, my father's private security that had no ties to the business. It was raining, and my father left the car and walked through the rain at a slow pace, ignoring the umbrella that was offered to him.

I followed him, soaked almost instantly.

My father dropped into an armchair in front of the fireplace and sat there, his elbow propped, his fingertips resting against his temple.

I stood and watched him, knowing he was so absorbed in his thoughts he had no idea I was there.

Minutes passed before I took the seat beside him.

His eyes were glued to the fire, not really seeing it.

"I'm sorry."

He gave no reaction, like he hadn't heard me. "I should have listened to you."

I studied the side of his face.

"I underestimated him."

I had no words to console him. Nothing to make this better. "We both walked out of there alive and unharmed. You've earned more money than you can spend in a lifetime. We should be grateful this is how it ended." Because it could have ended in a much worse way.

He said nothing.

"I think retirement will be good for you."

"Men like me don't retire, sweetheart."

"Then we can do something else. Open up a restaurant. Get into the wine business—"

"I spent my life building that business from the ground up. It contains my blood, sweat, and tears. A restaurant or a winery can't replace what I lost, the power and respect that I earned. No, I'm not going to sell pasta."

I shifted my gaze to the fire.

"I appreciate what you're trying to do, sweetheart." His eyes remained on the fire, never looking at me. "But I just want to be alone right now."

"Okay." I rose to my feet and left the seating area. When I looked at him again, he hadn't moved, remained parked in the armchair with his fingertips against his throbbing temple. I wanted to tell him I loved him, but I thought better of it and left.

8

AXEL

A week had passed.

The business was fully transferred to our possession, and we moved the products and teams to our own fulfillment centers. I suspected Dante would retaliate in some way, but all had been quiet on that front.

It was a promising new business venture for Theo and me, bringing in more money than all of our investments put together. The men who once served Dante seemed happy with the change, because we choose to be cooperative rather than vindictive. Dante thought leadership was about barking orders to your inferiors, when in reality, it was about guiding your team to success.

Theo stopped by my place so we could go over the numbers together, with scotch and cigars to celebrate. "Easiest money I've ever made." Theo tossed the sheet onto the coffee table. "He spent his life building this business, and we just—" he snapped his fingers "—took it like that. Fuck, that feels good."

It didn't feel good to me. I didn't take his business just from him—but Scarlett as well. Her ambition was to run it herself one day, to earn her own millions, to carry on her father's legacy with pride. I knew he had plenty of money to support her if she needed it, but I still felt like I'd stolen from her.

"Shouldn't you be happier about this?" Theo asked after he took a drink.

"The look on his face—fucking priceless," I said. "But the look on hers…makes me feel like shit."

"You spared his life for her."

"But she doesn't know that."

"She must. Why else would you let him live?"

I shrugged. "Because I'm a nice guy."

"That makes no sense."

"Well, she thinks I cheated on her and ghosted her, so it doesn't make sense that I did it for her."

"Then maybe you should tell her."

"I'm sure she wants to speak to me even less than she did before." I'd emasculated her father right before her eyes. She probably loathed me.

Theo regarded me for a while. "He got what was coming to him. Scarlett will be fine. She's smart and sexy. She'll have no problem bouncing back."

My eyes narrowed on his.

"Sorry, but she is."

I took a drink and let it slide.

My butler entered the parlor. "Sir, Dante has arrived and wishes to have a word with you."

"Ooh." Theo set down his glass. "The plot thickens."

My heart spiked when I heard what he said.

"You think he's here to beg?" Theo asked. "Or to try to kill you?"

"He almost shot me at the restaurant, but Scarlett reasoned with him." I still wondered if she'd done that for her father's benefit…or mine.

"Yeah," Theo said with a smirk. "I noticed that."

I turned to the butler. "Bring him in."

My butler gave a quick bow then walked off.

Theo slouched farther in the armchair. "Oh, this should be good. Vengeance—it's the gift that keeps on giving."

A moment later, Dante entered the room, wearing an olive-green jacket and dark jeans with loafers. His shoulders were sprinkled with drops of rain because the winter storms hadn't abated. He glanced at Theo, and the disdain on his face indicated he hadn't anticipated his presence.

"Just counting our coins." Theo raised his glass and took a drink.

Dante said nothing, but it was clear he had a lot to say.

I remained in the armchair, my chin propped on my knuckles. "What do you want?"

Dante eyed the unoccupied armchair before he took a seat. "Can we speak in private?"

I glanced at Theo.

Theo swirled his glass.

I shook my head. "I don't keep secrets."

A hint of frustration moved across his eyes. "Very well." His arms rested on the leather, and he crossed one leg over the opposite knee, making himself comfortable, like he'd been invited to this meeting. "I'm here to negotiate."

"Negotiate?" Theo was about to take a drink but snorted into the glass. "With what? You have nothing, Dante."

Dante kept his eyes on me. "This is why I wanted him gone, because he doesn't know when to shut his damn mouth."

Theo squeezed his glass before he downed the rest of the contents.

I knew what was about to happen, but I didn't stop it.

He threw the glass hard, hitting Dante right in the temple.

Dante grimaced as the glass hit the floor and shattered. A cut was immediately noticeable, but he didn't reach up to dab the blood.

I didn't like Dante, but I admired him for taking the hit without a squeal.

"Little bitch," Theo said. "Comes into *our* house like he's fucking invited..." His nostrils flared as he stared at Dante, who now had a streak of blood down the side of his face. "The only reason you've alive right now is because your daughter is your fucking guardian angel."

Dante looked at me, the blood dripping off his jawline onto his pants.

I grabbed a napkin from the table and tossed it at him. "Don't get blood on my shit."

He dabbed the cut then wiped up the side of his face before he crumpled the napkin into his closed fist. "Is that true?"

I thought that answer was obvious. "You'd be dead if you were anyone else."

He looked at the balled-up napkin soaked in blood in his hand for a moment before he dabbed at his temple again. "I built that business with my bare hands. I was a single father with no wealth, and all I wanted was a better life for my daughter. I built that empire to pass to her someday, and now I don't have that. Without it, I have no purpose...or worth."

"You have billions, Dante," Theo said. "With a *B*."

"It's not the same." His eyes remained on me, appealing to me and ignoring Theo. "I don't expect you to give it back to me entirely—"

"Or at all," Theo said. "There's nothing you could offer—"

I raised my hand to him. "Let us speak."

Theo took my glass off the table and started to drink that instead.

"I have something to offer both of you," Dante said. "If you cut me back in."

Theo kept his mouth shut this time, looking at me to speak.

"I won't sell the business to you." He couldn't afford to buy it anyway.

"I have something better than money." Dante continued to look at me. "For Theo, I will give you the other two skull rings. You'll have the full collection. And for you…" His eyes dropped, and he hesitated, like whatever he was about to say was as painful as bamboo shoots underneath his fingernails. "I'll give you my daughter."

Theo turned to stare at the side of my face.

I continued to look at Dante, whose eyes were on the floor in shame.

I savored the victory in silence. "You think I raped and beat my wife, but you want me to marry your daughter?"

His eyes remained down.

Theo piped up. "He asked you a question, asshole."

Dante was quiet for a long time, probably grappling with the self-loathing and the guilt. "I'll take back a third of the business, and upon my death or retirement, you'll absorb my share through your marriage to my daughter. My legacy will live on. My grandchildren will have the business I built on my own."

A distinct shiver moved down my spine at the thought of that ownership, to have Scarlett as mine, to fuck her, and then watch her have my sons and daughters. To have earned her after Dante's ruthless rejection.

"You still didn't answer the question," Theo repeated. "And no deal will be struck until you do."

Dante's eyes remained downcast. He was quiet for so long, it seemed as if he would never speak. But then finally, the words came. "She continues to speak highly of you." He raised his chin to look at me. "So I assume you treated her well."

I was fucking Prince Charming...except when I fucked her like the devil. "I would take your deal, except we have a problem." My fingers remained curled under my chin. "How will I get her to agree when she thinks I betrayed her?" I knew how proud she was, and even if she wanted to take me back, she wouldn't.

"I'll talk to her."

"You'll tell her that you forced me to do that."

Dante released a heavy breath. "No."

"Then we have no deal," I snapped. "Tell her the truth or walk away."

Dante slowly shook his head. "If I tell her the truth, I'll lose her. And I'd rather lose my business than my daughter."

I knew this wasn't a bluff. He manipulated her and used her, but I knew he genuinely cared for her. His ambition and greed only went so far.

"I'll talk to her," he said. "Convince her this is the only way."

It was still barbaric, treating her like a goat in a dowry, but since I was so close to having her, I didn't raise any objections.

"But you can never tell her what happened," he said. "And if you do, you know what the consequences will be. Just because I've lost my business doesn't mean I've lost my ability to get rid of people."

"You've got a lot of balls, threatening me right now."

"It wasn't a threat," he said calmly. "Just a reminder that our previous arrangement still stands."

"It wasn't an arrangement," I retorted. "It was coercion."

Dante paused, letting the tension pass. "Do we have a deal or not?"

My eyes shifted to Theo.

Theo gave a nod in agreement.

I turned back to Dante. "Yes. We have a deal."

9

SCARLETT

I had no purpose.

I used to wake up every morning and head to my father's estate to work. I visited the production sites, worked with the distributors, did all the paperwork. Time passed quickly, and before I knew it, I missed lunch.

But now…I had nothing to do.

My other passion was cooking, but I was too depressed for that. I worried about my father, knowing how hard he was taking this. He wouldn't be able to shake it off and move on. He was too emotionally invested in the business.

Axel's face was still burned in my mind. My heart had raced at the sight of him, but I'd probably failed to get a reaction out of him. Maybe he was still with Cassandra, or maybe he replaced her with someone else…and replaced her with someone else too.

Maybe that relationship meant a lot more to me than it ever did to him.

The thought stung so bad it almost brought tears to my eyes.

A knock sounded on the door.

My eyes immediately flicked to the entry. I was on the couch, a blanket over my legs, my hair in a high ponytail because I hadn't showered yet. Without anywhere to go or anything to do, I didn't feel the need to prepare to meet the day.

I opened the door and came face-to-face with my father. "Hey, Dad." It was unlike him just to stop by, but our reality had changed so dramatically that maybe this was our new normal. "What brings you here?"

He came in and kissed me on the cheek. "I was in the neighborhood and wanted to stop by." He didn't say anything about my dirty apartment, the pile of clean clothes on the couch that I hadn't bothered folding, or all the boxes and wrappers sitting on the kitchen counter. He took a seat away from the clothes and got comfortable.

"Sorry, wasn't expecting company."

He sat there for a while, his hands together in his lap as he looked at the painting on the wall.

"Everything alright?"

"Yes, everything is fine," he said calmly. "How have you been?"

"Kinda bored, to be honest."

He smiled, but it was disingenuous. "There's something I wanted to discuss with you."

"I'm listening."

He paused for a while. "One of the last things my mother said to me before she died was how proud she was. You know we grew up poor. I shared a room with two of my brothers until adulthood. When I bought her a villa…she looked at me in a way she never had. That moment was priceless, and I'll cherish it the rest of my life."

He'd told me that story multiple times, not because he thought I didn't know the tale, but just so he could tell it again. "Dad, even without the company, she would still be proud of you. They may have taken the business, but they didn't take your money. You're just as rich, and you can buy as many villas as you want."

"But I'm in my forties…and still have much to accomplish."

"I think you're being hard on yourself."

He looked away. "I wanted to give this business to you, Scarlett. I wanted it to be your inheritance."

"Dad, I've inherited better things from you. Like your heart and your courage."

His eyes remained averted, but they softened.

"I won't pretend I'm not disappointed by what happened, but all that matters is you and I are still here. We walked away unscathed, and I'm grateful for that."

"Well, I can't let it go so easily." He lifted his head and looked at me again. "So, I met with Axel last night and made a deal."

My entire body turned rigid at his words. "A deal?" I'd gotten the impression there wasn't room for a deal… just a takeover. Theo and Axel had plotted this from the beginning, and they'd gotten all their ducks in a row before they crushed my father.

"Yes. To get the company back."

"What did you offer them?" I asked. "Did you buy the company?"

"No. I offered Theo the other two skull rings."

"And what about Axel?" What did my father have that he would want?

He hesitated before he answered. "You…"

I stared at him blankly and waited for the rest of the sentence. "What does that mean?"

"He wants you to be his wife."

I heard the sentence and understood it, but it didn't make sense. It was like gibberish. "Excuse me?"

"I understand this may be overwhelming—"

"It's not overwhelming. It's just senseless."

"Marriage is the only thing he's willing to give us back the company in exchange for. I will get my portion, and then the business will be yours upon my death. You'll share it with him, but it'll be passed down to your children—"

"I'm waiting for the punch line to the joke," I said. "Because this must be a joke."

"You liked him—"

"Yes, *liked*. As in, past tense," I snapped. "No chance. He royally fucked that up. Honestly, I don't even understand why he would want me. He had me, and he walked away. Sounds like it's just a ploy to make you suffer."

"Whatever his angle is, I think we should do it."

"What?"

My father bowed his head and rubbed the back of his neck.

"You said you wanted me to marry someone who worships the ground I walk on. Now I have to settle for this pig."

"Men do stupid shit when they're young, sweetheart—"

"And I'm not going to do something stupid like marry him."

He lifted his head and looked at me. "There is no other way."

"We can live our lives."

My father released a heavy breath then let it out slowly. "I understand this is a lot to ask—"

"I told you not to cross Axel. I told you just to let things be, but you needed to be petty."

He closed his eyes for a brief moment. "You're right. I fucked up—"

"So now it's up to me to save our business by marrying a man I don't want? By marrying a man you hated so much that you backstabbed him?" It was ludicrous. "No. Fucking. Way."

My father turned quiet, dropping the argument. "I'm going to give you some time to think about it."

"I don't need to think about it, Dad."

"Well, if you don't…" He rubbed his hands together. "Everything I built will be gone. Overnight. As if decades of sacrifice and hard work never happened. Get me back our company, and I'll take care of Axel later."

My eyes narrowed on his face. "That's a joke, right? You underestimated him before, and you would underestimate him again? Do you ever learn your lesson?" I never spoke to my father this way, but I'd lost my sense after he asked me for this asinine favor.

"It's just an option if the marriage is unsuitable to you."

"I'm sorry, Dad. But I can't do it."

He gave a slight nod, his eyes full of disappointment. "I understand."

I could feel his emotion in his words, feel the sadness my answer caused. I shouldn't feel guilty for rejecting the proposal, but I did. "Let me think about it."

Slowly, life returned to his eyes, and a glimmer of a smile emerged on his face. "Thank you, sweetheart."

It'd been six months since I'd last visited his place.

When he'd tried to dump me, I came to his apartment and rode him on the couch, fighting for my man because I'd become so attached that I never wanted to let him go. He'd given me joy no other man would ever give me, and the thought of losing him had made me beside myself. But my art of seduction hadn't worked—because he was getting pussy elsewhere.

I couldn't believe I was back.

I almost chickened out and left when I stared at the gate.

But my father had laid out ridiculous terms to get our business back, and I had to verify their truths because there was no way that Axel wanted to marry me. There was no way that after six months of radio silence, he'd suddenly realized what he'd lost without saying a word to me.

I checked in with the guard then parked in his underground garage. News had probably traveled up the chain of command, and if Axel was home, he probably knew I'd parked beside his Maserati.

After I took a heavy breath, I stepped into the elevator then rose to the next level. My heart was like a drum in my chest, and my palms became so slippery that if I were holding my phone, it would probably drop.

The doors opened to the entryway, the round table with the beautiful flowers in the center. When I stepped onto the tile, my heels tapped and echoed. The place looked and smelled exactly the same, elegant but with masculine tones that made it clear a bachelor lived here.

His butler appeared. "I'll escort you to the parlor. Mr. Moreau is waiting for you."

Shit, this is happening. "Thank you."

He led the way, taking me to a part of the house I'd never been before. We moved through a couple hallways and passed a few windows before we entered the parlor, a sitting room with couches and armchairs in front of a fireplace on a nice rug. The coffee table had a bottle of wine and two glasses. The window in the rear showed the raindrops that were still stuck to the glass.

Axel sat in the armchair that faced me, in nothing but his sweatpants.

I hesitated as I stared at him, knowing he looked exactly as he had before, but maybe a little more cut. He used to walk around like that in my apartment, his ass tight under the fabric, his pants hanging low and showing off that sexy V formed by his hips.

I cleared my throat and took the seat across from him, the coffee table between us and the fire on my right.

The butler uncorked the wine and poured two glasses before he silently dismissed himself from the room.

Axel sat with his knees apart, one elbow propped on the armrest, his closed knuckles tucked underneath his hard chin. His eyes were so blue in that room full of mahogany and maroon with accents of gold and spots of gray. They stood out like a summer sky on a winter day. He didn't greet me with a single word or his signature smile.

I'd come all the way down here to speak to him, but now the words fell out of my head.

He remained quiet, his stomach flat and hard, his pecs still slabs of concrete. His arms were bulky with all the different muscles, and the cords that moved along his forearms, over his biceps, and then up his neck were so flexed, they looked like rivers on a 3-D map.

"My father told me you would give him back the business if I married you." I decided just to be candid about it, because I didn't know how to be diplomatic or strategic with this man, with this stranger, the mastermind who'd played my father for a fool. "Is that true?"

"I said I would give him back a *part* of the business, but yes."

Emotion constricted my chest because I didn't believe this could actually be true. My father must have misinterpreted the terms or even flat-out lied, because that seemed more believable than Axel actually wanting to marry me. But I guessed it was true. "Why?"

His gaze remained hard and unforgiving, and he stared at me with the stillness of a statue. "Because I want you."

I had a lot of retorts, but I swallowed them back for the sake of diplomacy. "You had me, Axel," I said calmly. "And then you dumped me for somebody else. A blonde with bigger tits." It took all my strength to sound normal, to hide the fact that I was still hurting all this time later. "So that's interesting."

He didn't respond to the allegations. Didn't even react to it.

I carried on. "You're a smart man, so you must have figured out there's no way in hell this is happening."

He lowered his fist from his chin and shifted his weight in the chair, his eyes still on me. "Then why are you here?"

"To negotiate."

"Your father and I already negotiated—"

"Now *we're* going to negotiate," I snapped. "When my father told me he was going to cut you from the business, I told him not to. I told him you were doing an excellent job, had gotten us out of a bad situation, and you deserved more loyalty than that. But my father couldn't see straight, because of what you did to me."

"Ironic. He said you wouldn't be able to be professional with someone you were involved with, but he's the one who couldn't be professional." This was the part where he was supposed to smile, but he rubbed his chin instead. "Even so, he fucked me over, and I feel no remorse for doing the same to him."

"He removed you as a distributor from *his* business. You taking that business is not an equal hit. You know it's not."

"He's done worse shit to me."

"Like?"

All he did was stare.

"Why won't you tell me?"

"It's best if you don't know."

"Why?"

"Because as much as I hate your father, I don't want you to hate him too."

What the fuck did he do?

"I'm not sorry for what I did. If your father wants back in, he has to meet my terms."

"But he can't force me to marry you," I insisted. "And as I said, that's not going to happen."

"Why?"

"Because I don't love you." The words felt heavy as they echoed off the impressive carved mantel beside us. They overshadowed the rain outside, which had picked up again out of nowhere. "And I won't marry someone I don't love."

He stared at me with those startling blue eyes, eyes that were so beautiful but also so deadly. "Theo says otherwise."

"Never once did I tell him I love you or ever loved you," I said. "So, he's full of shit—"

"But you're still hung up on me."

I laughed because it was absurd—and humiliating. "I've been with plenty of guys since you left me. Trust me, I'm not hung up on you." I looked him in the eye and forced a hostile stare, feeling the pain in my heart at the memory of those lonely nights, nights where I was left unsatisfied, nights where I'd slept with a guy I didn't even like just to feel better about Axel's rejection. "And that's pretty fucked up to have your *brother* date me to spy on me."

"That's not what happened."

"That's exactly what happened," I retorted. "He didn't ask me out because he wanted to."

"It's what your father wanted."

"He told Theo to ask me out?"

He nodded.

I rolled my eyes. "I don't believe you."

Axel stared at me in silence.

I waited for him to argue with me, but he let the conversation die. "My father's business means everything to him. I'm sure we can come to an arrangement without anyone getting married." I kept my back straight the entire time, protected my body with the armor of confidence, treated him like he was no one special. "We have connections in a lot of places. There must be something we can do for you."

"You came to me." His voice turned cold. "Because you needed me. I don't need you for anything. The business is mine, and I'm not giving up a share unless I get what I want."

My eyes narrowed. "That's barbaric."

He chuckled in a mocking way. "Your father is fucking barbaric. He asked you to agree to the plan. Why am I the only asshole here?"

"Because…"

His eyes narrowed. "Because what, baby?"

A surge of heat rushed through me, and not the good kind. "Don't ever call me that." It used to hug me like a blanket, but now it reminded me of the nights I cried in front of the TV, alone on the couch, in the dark. "You have no right to call me that." I evened out my voice to hide my emotion, to hide all the anguish that still scarred my heart.

"I'll call you that every night when you're my wife."

"I will *never* marry you." I raised my voice, all the ropes that bound my calmness shredding. "Fuck you, Axel. *Fuck. You.*"

His eyes watched me, remaining hard and emotionless. "I'm sorry for what happened. Really, I am. I've felt like shit about it every moment since then."

"Right."

"I mean that."

I avoided his look and stared out the window.

There was a long pause. "You have nothing else to offer me, Scarlett. Accept my conditions, and let's move forward."

My eyes flicked back to him. "You owe me."

His eyes narrowed. "I owe you?"

"When my father told me what you did, I believed you. I didn't look it up on the internet, and I still haven't. I had faith in the man I knew—and I maintained that faith without a shadow of a doubt."

The hardness in his eyes started to weaken.

"And then you stabbed me in the fucking back." My voice shook, but I controlled it, refusing to show any sign of tears. "When you tried to dump me, I assumed there was something I was missing, because the man I knew would never do that to me. I even asked my father if he'd said something to you, even though I knew he didn't, but because I believed in you, *in us*, so deeply."

His expression was different, focused and angry. "And what did he say?"

"No, of course."

His jaw clenched slightly before he rubbed his palm across his mouth.

"I stood by you when no one else did," I said. "You fucking owe me."

His eyes drifted away, and he seemed to be lost in thought because he ignored me.

"Axel."

He slowly turned back to me.

"You know I'm right," I said gently. "So please, give him back a fair portion."

He considered my words a long time, but he seemed far angrier than he had been at the start of this conversation. "You're right. You're the only woman who's ever trusted me so implicitly. And that's why I'm giving you the chance to get your business back—by marrying me. I have no desire to offer your father anything. Giving him a portion of the business is merely a gesture, and I can take it away whenever I feel like it. But when you're my wife, I can't take it away from you. It's legally yours."

The disappointment rushed through me.

"I already said you couldn't run this business on your own. You saw how Theo and I crossed your father, and he was none the wiser. If it weren't for you, I would have carved his eyes out with my butter knife." He cocked his head slightly and looked at me, like a king sitting on his throne in his palace. "A lot of horrible shit happens in this world, and you have no clue. You need someone like me to watch your back the way I watch my front. You need someone whom people respect and fear. You need a husband who will slit throats and break skulls for just looking at his wife the wrong way."

"Then how about I marry Theo instead?" I asked, just to get a rise out of him.

It worked—because his stare turned angry. "You don't love him."

"But I *could* love him. And there's no chance I would ever love you."

The fire filled the room with warmth, forcing the cold air back to the windows. It was quiet, the flames crackling in the hearth, the raindrops kissing the glass in the background. A few lamps were on in the corners, but overall, this was a dark room, with the exception of the fire. A heavy tension filled the space between us, his anger palpable but invisible.

After an endless silence and a vicious stare, he spoke. "Marry me—or lose your business."

"Wow, that's so romantic." I looked at the fire. "To have the chance to marry a cheating liar—"

"I didn't cheat on you."

"Sure."

"I didn't." He didn't raise his voice, but his anger was seething. "I wish you would trust me as you did before—"

"That trust is gone, Axel. Gone forever, never to return." I'd learned my lesson and would never forget it. "Maybe you did all those horrible things and I was too naïve to see it. I'm like that dumb woman who's the last to know her husband is fucking every woman he meets."

He was quiet, his face tinted red slightly, the cords in his neck popping.

"I should go." I rose to my feet. "This conversation is over."

Axel stared at me for a few more seconds before he got to his feet. Six-foot-something of muscles and tightness. He was a big man in the armchair, but now, he was a behemoth on his feet. He stayed on his side of the table as he stared at me, his hands sliding into the pockets of his sweatpants. "My offer still stands."

Those blue eyes used to stare at me all night. They used to make me feel cherished, feel secure, like there was no other woman who could even catch his eye. But now they made me feel empty…and broken. "Goodbye, Axel."

His reaction was subtle, but it was there. A quick grimace of hurt, his eyes closing to mask the pain of my words.

"I hope we never see each other again."

10

AXEL

I looked into my glass as I swirled the amber liquid, watching it spin around the square cubes of ice. The blocks tapped against the glass, music to my ears. I took a drink then repeated the process, swirling and staring. "She fucking hates me."

"Make her come and she won't."

I ignored Theo's comment. "Dante ruined my fucking life." I was tempted to throw the glass at the wall, but that would cause a scene, and the girls next to us would probably get scared.

"We can still kill him," he said. "If she hates you anyway, you might as well." He took a drink as he looked over his glass, eyeing the women across the bar.

I took another drink.

"Trust me, she's not over you."

"It seemed like she was."

"Whenever she talked about you, she became a different person."

"Because she was pissed off, Theo."

He took his eyes off the women and looked at me. "Trust me, I know this."

"Really?"

"I've pissed off a woman or two. Always got them back."

My glass was empty, and I tapped the counter so the bartender would make me another. I watched him grab the bottle and refill my glass, not needing to add more cubes since I downed it so quickly. He slid it back to me. "Were you caught with another woman?"

He hesitated. "No."

"Then it's not the same thing."

Theo's eyes drifted back to the women across the room. "Let's drink and fuck our troubles away. I know that works every time." He looked at me again. "We've got two admirers as we speak."

I kept my eyes on the contents of my glass. "She said she's slept around."

"What did you expect her to do?"

"I don't know. Tried not to think about it."

"You've been with other people."

"It was to scratch an itch, nothing more than that."

"It was probably the same for her," Theo said.

I swirled the glass.

"She'll come around. Her father wants his piece more than anything."

I took a drink. "Her decision seemed pretty ironclad."

"It was the first time you'd spoken since she saw you in that restaurant. Of course it's going to be a heated exchange. She needs to air out her grievances and let them stick before she can do anything else. Let her anger abate."

My phone vibrated in my pocket with a text, so I pulled it out to check. "Dante just texted me."

"What does that bitch want?"

I read the message before I said it out loud. "'I'll get her to change her mind. Just give me some time.'"

11

SCARLETT

I carried the bag of groceries to the counter and kicked the door shut behind me. The market was just a few blocks away, so it was convenient to grab what I needed on a daily basis since I could only carry so much at a time.

Now that I had a lot of free time, I focused on my cooking more. Tonight, I was making chicken, and I couldn't help but think of the first dinner I'd made Axel and how much he'd loved it. I hadn't cooked for anyone else since, except when I'd made those cannoli for Theo. I was irritated when he'd rejected me, but now that I knew he and Axel were close, it made sense.

The door opened, and my father entered. "Is it alright if I come in? I saw you walk into the building when I pulled up."

"Sure. I was just making dinner. Want to join?"

He shut the door then entered the kitchen, that warm smile on his face. "I can't say no to that. Do you need help?"

"Wash those vegetables. I'll take care of the chicken."

He washed his hands then got to work, washing the onion, carrots, and potatoes I'd left on the counter and then chopping and slicing on the cutting board. We fell into comfortable silence, the oven warming the room, the cold winter air pressing against the windows.

"What did you do today?" I asked after I rubbed the lemon marinade across the chicken.

"Worked out…read a book…took a nap."

"Took a nap?" I asked incredulously. "Wow, you're a whole different person."

"Yes, you could say that…" When he finished, he separated the veggies into different bowls so they would be prepared for when I needed them.

I transferred the chicken into a deep baking dish and then arranged the veggies around. It was the same meal I'd made for Axel. I hadn't made it in over six months, and I thought it was time to move on. I placed it in the oven and set the timer. "Want some wine?"

"I'd love some."

I uncorked a bottle and poured two glasses.

He took a seat at the table, and I joined him.

We sat there together for a while, neither of us addressing what we were both thinking.

He swirled his glass before he sipped it. "How was your day?"

"About the same. I went to the gym, went to the market."

"No nap?" he teased.

I chuckled. "No nap."

He smiled, but it quickly disappeared as he looked into his glass. "Sweetheart—"

I already knew what he was about to say based on his tone alone. "I'm not going to marry him."

His eyes remained on his wine.

"Just being in the same room as him…was insufferable."

He didn't say anything.

"There's more to life than work."

"And for some people, life is work. And that's us." He lifted his eyes and looked at me, his fingers pinching the stem of his glass. "It's more than work. It's something that we built. It's ours."

Now I was the one who looked down at my wine.

"I know how much you wanted it, Scarlett. I saw you bust your ass every day to prove that you were worthy of the keys to the kingdom. And you're prepared to just let it go? Let someone else take what is rightfully yours?"

I continued to focus on my wine.

"Marry him. Bide your time. And then hurt him the way he hurt you."

My eyes lifted to meet his.

"He crossed us. Now, let's cross him."

"I don't see how we can accomplish that—"

"It'll take time. A lot of patience. But eventually, we'll see an opening and take it. We'll remove him from the business and take it as ours."

I continued to stare at him.

"Come on, sweetheart."

"He said he would kill you if you retaliated."

"It's a bluff. He won't kill me."

"Why?"

He stared. "Because he would have done it already if he could. And he certainly won't kill you. We have the blood of Romans in our veins. We don't let someone take our kingdom. We fight to take it back."

I looked at my wineglass again, my heart thumping harder than before.

"Make him pay for what he's done to you—to us."

I typed the message, deleted it, and then retyped it. It sat there for a couple minutes before I sent it, unsure if I'd just made a strategic move—or doomed myself. *Let's talk.*

The three dots appeared instantly, like he'd been staring at his phone when the message came through. *Let's.*

I'll meet you at Le Conte at 7.

It's a date.

I ignored his last message and locked the screen. There was a painful pit in my stomach, an unease that no amount of wine would drown. My nerves were balled into knots, and that made a flush of dread flow through me. I thought I could do this, but a simple text exchange was enough to make me lose my balance.

At seven, I arrived at the restaurant, wearing a black dress with matching heels, my heavy coat keeping me insulated from the cold outside. I uncinched the sash and opened the buttons before my coat was taken. Axel had already arrived, so the hostess guided me to his table.

He sat there alone, in dark jeans and a button-up with the sleeves pushed to his elbows. His eyes were focused out the window before he turned to look at me, his pupils dilating slightly at the sight of me. He gave me a quick glance over without hiding it, like he didn't care if I saw him check out my figure in the skintight dress.

I sat across from him, and a bottle of wine was already on the table.

He grabbed the bottle and poured my glass then he relaxed in the chair, his blue eyes locked on mine with that intensity he used to show all the time. He showed it when he stared at me across a crowded room, when we had dinner together, when I sat across from him in the bathtub. He did it now, as if nothing had changed.

I grabbed the glass and took a drink. "Thanks for meeting me."

"The pleasure is mine." His elbows rested on the armrests, and his big hands came together, old scars over his knuckles. The cords moved up his forearms and disappeared under his pushed-up sleeves. His hair was a little longer than it used to be, combed back and out of his face.

I was the one who had asked him to meet me, but the words struggled to form on my tongue.

He seemed content to sit in silence and stare.

Since I was the one who'd called this meeting, he probably felt no obligation to speak until he knew what I wanted from him. "Why do you want to marry me?"

"I already answered this question."

"Then give me a different answer, because that one was bullshit."

A glimmer of a smile moved on to his lips and reached his eyes. "You're spicier than I remember."

"I just have a lower tolerance for lies and deceit."

The smile disappeared. "I meant what I said." His intense stare returned. "I want you."

"Then fuck me for a night," I retorted. "Why does it have to be marriage?"

His fingers slid together as his hands rested against each other. "If it was just a night, would you say yes—"

"Yes."

He stilled, giving a nod so subtle his head barely moved. "Tonight?"

"Sure."

His thumbs started to move together.

"Sex is a much smaller payment than marriage," I said. "So, how about we do that instead? We have our dinner then go back to my apartment and do whatever the fuck you want. Then tomorrow, you return the business to us and disappear."

"Do whatever the fuck I want…" He turned his eyes away, and a smirk moved across his lips. "Fuck, you're killing me."

"Then take the deal."

He continued to let his eyes sit on something else in the room, his mind thinking. "That's a very uneven trade—"

"No condom." I could deal with Axel for a night. Could go through the motions to save the business—and get an orgasm or two along the way.

His eyes shifted back to me, and he gave a heavy sigh. "Baby, you know your audience—"

"Call me that again, and I'm walking out of here."

He started to massage his knuckles. "As enticing as that is…no deal."

The disappointment was so potent, it was actually painful.

"My offer stands."

"If all you want is to fuck me, then why marriage—"

"I never said all I wanted was to fuck you. I said I wanted you—and that meant all of you."

"And why would you want that?" I snapped.

He paused before he answered, his expression hardening. "Because these past six months have been the shittiest of my life."

I stared as I felt the rage explode inside me. It wasn't romantic. It wasn't endearing. "How's Cassandra doing?" I was so mad that it just came out, firing bullets without truly aiming.

"I haven't spoken to her since that night."

"Since you fucked her."

"I didn't fuck her—"

"I can't have a conversation with you if you're just going to lie."

He stared for a long time before he released a heavy sigh. "I've thought about you every day these last six months. What happened between us was…a very shitty sequence of events, and this time apart has only shown me how much you mean to me. I fucking miss you."

I wouldn't let his words worm their way into my heart and poison my mind. "You know, most guys send flowers and a card."

"I know you," he said quietly. "I know you'll never take me back—"

"Damn right."

"So this is the only way I get what I want."

"To marry a woman who hates you?"

"You don't hate me," he said quietly. "I understand I hurt you and you're angry, but I know you don't hate me."

I wanted to tell him I despised him, that I'd never hated someone so much in my life, fire off insults left and right…but I couldn't. Despite what he did, I still cared about him, which was fucking pathetic.

"Marry me, and you get what you want."

I was quiet.

He stared like he'd just proposed and waited for an answer.

The waiter came over and pushed the tension away like it was a cloud of smoke.

Axel ordered for himself then ordered me the gnocchi, as if he knew I wasn't really hungry anyway, so whatever he ordered was just fine.

The waiter disappeared.

"You wouldn't be here if you weren't receptive to the idea." He reached into his pocket and withdrew a small box.

My heart quickened.

He popped it open and pulled out a ring. A platinum band with a princess cut diamond in the center. He reached across the table slightly and placed it in front of me so I could see it outside the box, see the way it glittered under the chandelier.

I glanced at it for half a second before I looked at him again.

His eyes had darkened back to their earlier intensity. "Marry me."

I didn't touch the ring. I had no intention of letting it come near me. "How would this marriage function?"

"What do you mean?"

"Would we be monogamous—"

"Yes."

"Because I'm receptive to an open marriage, especially since you have a wandering eye—"

"No." He clenched his jaw as he answered me. "It's just you and me."

"I would rather have realistic expectations—"

"I only want you, Scarlett." His stare deepened.

The stare became too much, so I looked down at the ring then returned it to him.

He didn't take it.

I set it down in front of him before I leaned back in my chair. "Do you want children?"

"Yes."

"How many?"

"As many as you're willing to give me."

"How would the business work?"

"You can do what you do now, run the numbers, take care of bookkeeping and appointments. I'll handle all the physical stuff."

"And my father?"

"He and I will have to discuss that."

The plan had been laid out, but it was hard to swallow. The attraction was still there, but it was masked by a twisted pain in my stomach. I'd never forget the way my heart had dropped when I'd seen him walk past with Cassandra, when he pulled out the chair for her the way he did with me. I went home and cried so hard I gave myself a migraine—probably the very moment he was screwing her.

How could I ever let him touch me again?

"We sleep in separate rooms," I said.

"No."

"That's not up for negotiation. Take it, or we have no deal."

He was quiet, mulling over the situation in silence. "You'll fuck me but won't sleep with me?"

"Sex is meaningless. Who you sleep beside every night…that's intimate. I'm not doing that with you. It's ridiculous that I have to make this sacrifice just to have what's mine. You're taking everything from me, but I'm not letting you take that."

He stared at me from across the table in silence, his fingers brushing over his lips as he became lost in thought. "So, we have a deal, then?"

It made me sick to say it. "Yes."

He closed his eyes for an instant and released a breath, like he'd been holding it this whole time. He looked at the ring in front of him and picked it up.

"I'm not wearing that until I have to."

He returned the ring to the box and put it back in his pocket. His expression hardened once more as he stared at me, his presence large enough to cross the table and touch me.

The waiter arrived with our dishes.

"I'm sorry, but can I have this to go?" I asked. "Something came up."

"Of course." The waiter left to retrieve a takeout container.

"You're going to marry me but won't have dinner with me?" he asked, his voice hurt.

"Yep."

The waiter returned with the container and set it down.

I grabbed it and placed my dinner in the box before I closed it up. "Goodnight, Axel."

He said nothing as he watched me get up, the steam rising from his hot dish.

I walked off and waited for him to stop me.

But he didn't.

12

AXEL

We sat there in the parlor, smoking and drinking, waiting for our guest to arrive.

"You got the answer you wanted," Theo said. "That's all that matters."

I stared at the cigar between my fingertips, watching the smoke slowly rise to the ceiling. "It's not the fairy tale I hoped it would be. Wouldn't even have dinner with me."

"She thinks you lied and cheated, Axel. How else do you expect her to react?"

I continued to stare at the cigar.

"It's gonna take time. If you aren't going to vindicate yourself with the truth, you'll have to win her over the hard way. Which is going to take a lot of time. And a lot of fucking patience."

I brought the cigar to my mouth and let the smoke fill it again, the taste of licorice distinct on my tongue. Then I pushed it out from between my lips before I took a drink of the scotch.

"You can do it, Axel."

My butler entered the parlor. "Dante has arrived. Shall I show him in?"

"Yes."

He gave a quick bow then left.

Theo refilled his glass and got comfortable in the armchair.

It had been in this very room that Scarlett had shown up unannounced and we'd faced each other for the first time in six months. I'd seen her at the restaurant, but it wasn't as intimate as that night. The rain had pelted the windows, and I'd looked at those lips I longed to kiss.

Dante entered the parlor a moment later, the cut still visible on the side of his temple.

I wondered if Scarlett had asked him about it.

Dante greeted us both with eye contact before he took a seat. His arrogance had been stripped away by siege, and now he was a quiet little bitch like I wanted him to be. He crossed his leg and rested his ankle on the opposite knee.

"Scarlett said yes." I felt a thrill at the thought because I'd been reflecting on our memories together, the way she made me feel, the way she kissed me like I meant the world to her. I wanted that again…desperately. I knew it wouldn't be that way, at least not for a while, not unless I gave her a reason to trust me when I'd never broken that trust to begin with.

"She told me."

"How did you change her mind?" Her rejection had been venomous, spiteful. But somehow, she'd had a change of heart—or, at least, a change of mind.

"I reminded her how important that company is to us. I told her we were Romans—"

"And the Romans were overthrown by the barbarians," I said. "I guess that makes me a barbarian."

He did his best to keep a calm composure, but the anger shone through just a bit. "Through marriage, Rome still rules." His arms moved to the armrests.

"She'll outlive you. And her children will outlive you both. We take back the throne—with a hint of barbarian blood."

He talked about the business like it was a dynasty for the history books, but no illegal activity would have a legacy like he thought it would. The only people who would remember it would have a quick death. "She wants to resume her position. I'll take care of everything else. She won't be attending meetings or counting ounces like you had her do before. That was reckless and stupid."

Dante said nothing. "And what will I do?"

"Production," I said. "With Theo's connections, we've expanded this business, but in order to maintain it, we need product. A lot more of it. Make that happen."

"I can hire more guys," he said. "Get a bigger facility."

"Increase external shipment," I said.

"That's a challenge," Dante said. "To move that much product across the border and then move it again…" He shook his head. "Once my production partners figure out the kind of revenue we've reached, they're going to sell the product directly and cut us out entirely. We need to be completely self-reliant."

"And if they do that," Theo said, "they get shot in the back of the head. It's that simple."

"It's hard to control what the Colombians do—"

"I control what everyone does." Theo brought the glass to his lips and took a drink.

"Is Scarlett planning the wedding?" I wanted to text her, call her, carry on with the relationship that was paused too soon, but I knew my advances would be unwelcome. I had to take it slow or risk pushing her away altogether.

"We assumed you would do it at the town hall," Dante said. "Just get it done."

"This is the only wedding she's ever going to have, and she wants to do it at the town hall?" I asked incredulously.

Dante leaned back in the chair. "It's the middle of winter—"

"I'll marry her in the rain. I don't give a shit."

Dante looked away in discomfort. "This is something you should discuss with her. I'm not involved in this sort of thing." He looked at the bottle of scotch, like he could really use a drink. "Let's talk business. That's all I'm really interested in—"

"Yes, I know you don't give a shit about your daughter," I snarled. "I'm fully aware."

Now Dante's face started to tint. "I find that deeply offensive."

"It's supposed to be offensive."

He paused, chewing the inside of his cheek. "I'm always looking out for what's best for her—"

"I was best for her, and you took me away."

He sighed. "You have her now—"

"It's not what it used to be, and it probably never will be," I snapped. "Because she thinks I would treat her like that. Let me tell her, and we'll have the wedding we both want—"

"Never."

The words died in my throat, knowing he would never budge. "Until we're married, there's no business to discuss. You can go."

Annoyance swept across his gaze like a closing curtain. "Axel—"

"I said go."

He remained in the chair, trying to think of what to say, but when nothing good came to mind, he rose from his chair and let himself out.

I wanted to show up on her doorstep, but I knew coming to her residence unannounced wouldn't be welcome. So, I texted her. *I'd like to speak with you.*

Her dots showed up instantly. *What?*

In person.

Unless you're showing me a PowerPoint presentation, we can speak over the phone.

So we can speak in person when you want to, but not when I want to?

Yep. That's what happens when you stick your dick in someone else.

I almost chucked the phone at the wall. So fucking infuriating. *I'm coming by. See you in 20.*

I won't open the door.

Like that will stop me. I left my place and drove to hers. I knew she'd moved a couple months ago. Found that out by chance. It was a bigger place on a nicer street. There was a garage underneath the building to park her car. I preferred it to the building where she'd lived before, so I was pleased by the news.

I took the stairs to her floor then stopped in front of her door. I tried the knob and was pleased to see that it was unlocked, so I let myself inside. The living room was larger, there was a big TV on the wall, new furniture and decor, and her kitchen was far more spacious. It was a chef's kitchen, with an island, a large sink, and two ovens.

She stood at the counter, working on something for dinner.

I could smell it the second I walked in the door. All the spices and flavors melded together in a savory scent. My chef cooked for me, but he couldn't replicate her work, which was fucking exquisite. When I'd told her to become a chef, it wasn't false praise. "Something smells good."

She didn't look up, even though she knew I was there. She put on her oven mitts and set the tray inside the oven before she closed the oven door. She was in a loose sweater with black leggings, her long hair in a braid to stay out of her face. There was no makeup on her face because she hadn't expected company, and even though she'd had twenty minutes to put it on before I came, she didn't, because she didn't care how she looked.

"You left the door unlocked."

"I didn't want to sleep without a door."

"I would have fixed it for you if I'd broken it."

"Ah, that's so sweet." She hadn't looked at me once since I'd been there. She reached for a bottle of wine and poured two glasses. "It's so nice to have a good man around."

Her sarcasm felt like an insult.

"Why are you here?" She leaned against the counter and looked at me for the first time, her ankles crossed.

My eyes locked on hers, admiring that beautiful neck and those full lips. It was hard to look at her without staring. But that was all I wanted to do…stare. I used to watch her sleep beside me. Used to watch her relax in the bathtub. Some people cherished paintings and sculptures, but she was my art.

"We need to discuss the wedding."

"You want roses or lilies?" Her eyes were ice-cold.

"We aren't doing this at the town hall."

Her eyebrows furrowed like she couldn't believe what I'd just said. "Then what's your idea?"

"A real wedding."

"Why?"

"Because this is the only wedding I'm ever going to have," I said. "I'm not the most romantic guy, but I'm not getting married in jeans."

"You can wear a suit to the town hall—"

"I know you want that, too."

"Yes, for a real marriage—"

"This is a *real* marriage—"

"It's fucking coercion." She grabbed the glass on the counter beside her and took a big sip.

"Let's get married at the church," I said. "Have the reception at the Four Seasons."

She stared at me and took another drink.

"We can probably have it planned within a month."

She looked thoroughly disinterested. "Are you asking me to plan it?"

"I assumed you would want to—"

"I want to sign a sheet of paper in jeans. You're the one who wants all this."

"Fine," I said. "I'll hire someone to do it for us."

"Great." She took a drink of her wine again before she moved to the dining table and took a seat.

I grabbed the extra wineglass and took the seat beside her.

She drank from her glass as she looked out the window, the world dark and cold.

I stared at the side of her face, wishing I could just tell her the truth, have her look at me the way she used to. She didn't hate me, but she seemed indifferent to me, and that was somehow worse.

"Is there something else you wanted to discuss?" Her eyes remained directed out the window.

"Is my place okay? Or did you want to move elsewhere?"

"Is your place okay for what?"

"For us to live."

She stared down at her wineglass and slowly traced the rim with her fingertip. "I'm keeping my apartment."

"To rent out?"

"No," she said simply. "To live."

I stared hard at the side of her face. "That's not how this is going to work."

"You said we didn't have to sleep together."

"Begrudgingly," I retorted. "And I assumed you meant a different bedroom in the house."

"What does it matter if it's in the same house—"

"Because we're husband and wife. I can't protect you if I'm not with you."

"I don't need your protection—"

"Yes, you do," I snapped.

Her eyes returned to the window.

"I'd appreciate it if you chose to embrace this rather than resist it."

"You want me to embrace a marriage I'm being forced into with a man who broke my fucking heart?" She turned to look at me, and the mirage of emptiness was shattered by the emotion in her eyes. "You want me to be excited to be with a man who has no respect for me? A man who could dump me and replace me overnight?" She turned back to her wine. "Lucky me."

I closed my eyes and rubbed my temple, self-loathing I didn't deserve washing over me. "Scarlett."

She didn't look at me.

I wished I could fucking tell her. Tell her that her father was the one who had no respect. "I'm so sorry for hurting you. You have no idea how much it hurts me to listen to you say all of that." To be unaware of the truth, to think I would ever replace her with anyone else, that the one person she could trust was the one she'd been taught to despise.

As if my words meant nothing to her, she took a drink.

"I will spend the rest of my life making it up to you."

She focused on her wine instead of me.

"Scarlett—"

"You can't make it up to me, Axel."

"I can if you let me."

Her finger returned to the rim of her glass, and she traced it.

"Scarlett—"

"I thought you were different. Maybe that's why it hurt so much…because I really believed that. But I should have known that a man so sexy and kind was too good to be true, that you would be like all the others, distracted by the next piece of ass."

It took all my strength to keep my mouth shut. I continued to protect my parents when they didn't deserve my protection, but they also didn't deserve to die either.

She turned cold again, her voice defeated. "Let me know the details about the wedding. I'll be there." She finished off the rest of her glass then walked back to the counter to refill it. But then she leaned against the island, her ankles crossed, and sipped her wine as she waited for me to leave.

I remained in the chair, my body too heavy to lift.

She stared elsewhere, the silence of the apartment pierced by the sound of the oven.

I finally got to my feet and faced her.

She wouldn't look at me.

There were things I wanted to say, confessions I wanted to make. I wanted her to know how much she meant to me, the depth of my feelings, the memories that stayed with me all these months later. But I knew she would reject every one of them. "I'll let you know the details."

13

SCARLETT

I lied to my friends about Axel. Told them we got back together and we were eager to get married. I couldn't tell them the truth, that it was all business and corruption. We went to pick out my dress from the bridal boutique, and what should have been one of the greatest days of my life turned out to be one of the most meaningless.

I didn't care what Axel thought when he saw me in it. I didn't care if he thought I was beautiful. I didn't care what anyone thought, because this wedding wasn't real, at least not to me. It was just a means to an end, and at some point, my father and I would figure out a way to cut him out of our lives and take back the crown.

I would remarry someday, and that would be the real wedding.

I picked out a dress, the seamstress took my measurements, and then we left the store to get dinner. I always had a good time with my friends, but in light of what we were celebrating, I found it hard to live in the moment. Instead of starting a new life, I felt like I was losing my old one.

I returned to my apartment alone and opened another bottle of wine. Axel wouldn't allow our participation in the business until I married him, so my father and I had nothing to focus on. I spent my time drinking. I wasn't sure what my father did.

I was on the couch when Axel texted me. *Did you pick out your dress?*

I rolled my eyes at his message. *Yes.*

Is it slutty? He sent one of those smiling emojis with the sunglasses.

I set the phone aside and ignored him.

Time passed so quickly when there was something to dread.

I dreaded this wedding with every fiber of my being, so of course, time seemed to be moving at double the speed, mornings and afternoons becoming a blur, the hours escaping so fast it seemed like I had a time machine.

I had a constant stitch in my chest now, a tightness that wouldn't abate, a heaviness to my heart that made it hard to stand. It was time for me to start packing up my belongings so Axel's men could pick everything up, but I hadn't even started.

The rehearsal dinner was tomorrow, and I'd run out of time.

All I could do was sit on the couch and think about the way my life had turned out. I'd expected to fall in love with the most amazing guy and have a beautiful family. I'd expected him to be a great husband and an even better father. But those dreams were ridiculous fantasies, because I was marrying a man who broke me. A man I couldn't trust. And I was doing it for the wrong reasons.

The rehearsal dinner arrived.

I wore a black cocktail dress. Thought the color was appropriate because I felt like my soul had died. My father and I pulled up to the church, and he got out first but I stayed behind.

When he came around to the other side to get me, I stayed in my seat.

He watched me before he rested his forearm on the door. He didn't say anything, just gave me time to adjust to reality, that I had to walk into that building and rehearse marrying a man who had left permanent scars across my heart.

It was a cold evening, the wind entering the car and causing bumps to appear on my arms.

My father continued to stare at me. "It's alright, sweetheart." His hand went to my shoulder.

His touch seemed to give me new life, because I managed to get out of the car and take his arm as we walked into the church. It was empty except for us, rows of pews with the golden statues at the front. It was a beautiful church, old and historic, the ceiling hundreds of feet high.

People were already there. Some of Axel's men and his friends.

My friends were there too, ready to rehearse a wedding I didn't even want to have.

Axel's eyes found mine across the room, and he stared like he always did, stared so hard it carved into my skin.

I left my coat on because I was cold, my arm still through my father's.

Axel crossed the room and approached me, dressed in slacks and a button-up shirt, his sleeves pushed to his elbows. One look at my father made him disappear. Then Axel extended his hand to me, his strong eyes locked on mine.

I felt the stares of everyone around us. Some people knew this was fake and some people didn't, so their perception of this moment was probably polarizing.

He spoke with a gentle voice. "Come on, you can do this."

I stared at his hand before I finally took it. It was the first time I'd touched him, and to my horror, I felt a flash of emotion, of electricity, even warmth. My eyes remained down so he wouldn't know what I felt.

But he squeezed my hand—like he did know.

The dinner was held at my father's house, with drinks and appetizers in the parlor and then dinner in the dining room. With red cheeks from the wine and booze, everyone laughed and had a good time. My father did too, talking with his brother and his wife, boasting about how excited he was that his little girl was getting married.

It was such a shitty night.

I avoided Axel most of the time, and after the rehearsal, that was easy to do because he wasn't around much. He wasn't in any room that I walked into, wasn't talking to any of his friends, completely absent.

Then I looked out the window into the night and saw Axel and Theo sitting outside, at the very table where Axel and I used to talk, and they each smoked a cigar as they thrived in the cold, neither of them wearing jackets.

I drank my wine as I stared at them, wondering what they were talking about. I watched Theo pat Axel on the shoulder before he put out his cigar and came inside. When the door opened, the cold air flooded into the house as a draft, and then a moment later, it was warm again.

Axel remained alone outside, and I wondered if he was having second thoughts.

When Theo saw me staring out the window, he came to my side. "His parents refuse to come to the wedding. He's taking it pretty hard." He stared at Axel with me, his body inches from mine. "I'm sure he could use some company." He gave me a hard look before he turned and rejoined the party.

I stared at the back of Axel's head, seeing him slouched in the cold, metal chair, the smoke rising from his mouth to the cold sky. His glass of scotch was there too, the air so frigid that the ice cubes didn't melt.

I grabbed my coat from the rack then walked outside.

He turned his head at the sound of my heels, probably expecting anyone but me to brave the weather to join him. His stare was hard at first, but it slowly softened at the sight of me, and he looked a little surprised. He pulled out the chair for me without getting out of his and then put out his cigar.

I bundled the coat right around me and cinched the sash at my waist. "You don't have to do that."

"It's rude to smoke in front of a lady."

"I really don't mind."

"Well, I do." He grabbed his glass and took a drink before he stared at the fountain and the olive trees on the property. A string of white lights was strung across the terrace, and there was a fire pit in the center, but it was too far away to provide warmth.

We sat in silence.

I wasn't even sure why I'd come out here.

He drank and didn't make small talk, his mood sour.

"Theo said your parents aren't coming."

He stared straight ahead. "I knew they wouldn't. I'm not sure why I bothered asking."

I looked at the side of his face, seeing the hardness of his jawline, the vapor of his breath that disappeared into the dry air. "I would want my father there, even though this isn't real."

He stared at his glass for a moment before he looked at me, his blue eyes deep and broken. "It's real to me." As if we were back in time, he looked at me the way he used to, like he could stare at me forever.

When I couldn't handle the look anymore, all the pain it caused me, I glanced away. "I'm sorry they won't be there tomorrow."

"I wanted them to meet you." He looked forward again, returning his glass to his lips. "They would have loved you, and I think you would have liked them, if this were five years ago." He took another drink, leaving the glass empty. "There are days when I'm fine with it, and there are other days when I'm not fine with it. I'm sure you can figure out what kind of day this one is."

"I'm sorry."

He inhaled a slow breath then let it out. "I know you are, baby."

I didn't tell him not to call me that, not now, not when he was so sad. "They'll come around eventually."

He stared at his empty glass for a long time. "I don't think they will. But thanks for trying to make me feel better."

The wedding day arrived.

I skipped dinner the night before and breakfast today, but I still felt like I was going to hurl.

If Axel had asked me to marry him before he'd broken my heart, I probably would have said yes even though our relationship had only lasted two months. But now, it felt wrong. It felt like a cage with steel bars and three locks on the door.

I got ready, had someone do my hair and makeup, and stared at my ghostly white face in the mirror. My dress fit a little loose, as if I'd somehow lost weight since my last fitting two weeks ago. But not eating day after day would do that.

I got ready in my room at the Four Seasons, the honeymoon suite that Axel and I would share tonight as husband and wife. Once I was finished, the car took me to the church, into a private room where I would wait until all the guests had arrived, and the ceremony would begin.

I really felt like I would throw up.

It was a small room with a few couches and armchairs around a coffee table. The window outside showed the gray winter sky that was somehow so bright it made me squint. My dress had lace sleeves to minimize the cold, and it had a sweetheart top before it stretched down into a mermaid skirt. It was a beautiful gown, an expensive purchase that my father was happy to cover, but I felt like an impostor wearing it.

The door opened, and my father stepped inside. "Sweetheart." His eyes were glued to me, and he hesitated before he came closer. "You…you look beautiful."

I rose to my feet so he could see me fully, because he hadn't seen the dress that I picked out. "Thank you." A diamond necklace was around my throat, a gift my father had given me a few years ago. I'd never felt so beautiful and so miserable at the same time.

He came closer and gave me a smile. "We've got a full house out there. Everyone came."

"That's great." I couldn't care less.

He watched me, his smile slowly failing. "I know this is hard, but you're doing the right thing."

"Am I?" I whispered.

He lowered his voice, as if someone might be listening. "It's just for a short while."

"How long?"

"A couple months…a year. Hard to say."

A couple months with someone you didn't trust felt like a lifetime.

"For what it's worth, I think Axel truly cares for you."

"He has a funny way of showing it."

He brought me in for a hug, his cheek resting against mine. He held me there, and it was the first time I'd felt at peace in three days. He seemed to know I needed it because he kept me there for a long time. "I'll be waiting for you out there." He pulled away and gave me a kiss on the temple.

"Alright."

He stepped out and shut the door behind him.

The second he was gone, all the agony returned. It was just me alone in that room, terrified to face the future waiting outside for me. My bouquet was on the table in the water-filled vase, ready for me to take, but I turned to look out the window instead.

14

AXEL

Twenty minutes passed, and Scarlett didn't emerge.

The music didn't start, and the guests started to chat louder, their voices echoing off the walls and the glass ceiling, growing restless.

"Maybe I should check on her."

Theo stood beside me, my best man. "Maybe she ran."

I turned to look at him, about to dismiss the idea, but then my heart fell into my stomach. "Come on." We walked down the aisle at a normal pace so no one would know that the bride had probably taken off.

We made it into the hallway where Dante was waiting.

"Where is she?" I blurted.

"I spoke to her a bit ago," Dante said. "She seemed upset. I calmed her down. I think she just needs—"

"It's locked." Theo moved ahead and tried the door. "Scarlett?"

No response.

Theo turned to me and raised his arms. "We've got a runaway bride."

"Fuck."

Dante genuinely looked surprised, so I knew this wasn't part of his plan. "I would call her, but…" He reached into his pocket. "She asked me to hold her phone."

"Theo, grab the car."

Theo took off to bring the car to the front.

I turned to Dante. "Stall. I'll get her back."

He rubbed his temple and sighed. "Please find her."

I walked out the door and made my way to the curb right as Theo turned the corner and pulled up in front, the engine loud.

I hopped inside, and he took off.

"How are we supposed to find her?"

"Drive around and search for a woman in a wedding dress." She had no money and no phone, so she must be walking down the street, dirtying her gown on the street.

Theo drove fast, whipping around the roundabouts and turning back up different streets. Several minutes passed, and there was no sign of her. "You think she took the bus?"

"Fuck, I don't know."

We continued to drive, the search starting to turn hopeless.

But then Theo rounded the corner, and I spotted her, standing in the freezing cold outside a café, passersby on the street staring at her in her gown. "There. Pull over."

Theo cut off a car to get to the curb. The cars honked back and forth, but I was too focused on Scarlett to care. I hopped out of the car, and Theo took off again because he couldn't park the car there.

She didn't even notice me, standing there with nowhere to go. Her apartment was clear across town, and it would take her hours to walk back in those heels.

"Scarlett."

She turned at the sound of her name and nearly jumped out of her skin. "Jesus…"

I undid my jacket then wrapped it around her.

She must have been cold because she didn't throw it on the ground or scream at me. "I can't do it." She wouldn't look at me, tightening the coat around herself to lock the warmth against her body. "I just can't."

My hands went to her arms, getting close to her. "It's okay."

Her eyes lifted to mine, the surprise written across her features.

"Let's go inside and get a coffee."

"What?"

"Come on." I took her hand and opened the door for her. The café was empty because it was the middle of the day, between lunch and dinner, when everyone was out or enjoying a nap. I took her to a table in the corner.

She sat down and tightened the coat around her, her face pale from the stress and the cold. I went to the counter, ordered a couple coffees and pastries, and then returned to the table when I had everything.

I set the latte in front of her along with the vanilla scone, all they had left.

She cupped the mug with both hands to feel the warmth then took a drink. Slowly, the unease started to slip away as she enjoyed her coffee. She picked at the scone, taking a few bites as she kept her eyes down.

I didn't press her with questions or pressure her to return to the church. I just let her breathe.

She continued to pick at the scone, eventually eating all of it and leaving only a few crumbs behind. "I haven't eaten anything since yesterday."

"How was it?"

"Loaded with sugar and fat…so it was fucking delicious."

I grinned before I took a drink.

She turned to look out the window on the other side of the café, and reality seemed to come back to her because she released a heavy sigh. "This isn't how I pictured this day." Her voice dropped, full of solemnity. "I wanted to get married outside in the summer, not in a church during the wettest winter we've ever had. I wanted to marry a man I could trust with my life, who would never hurt me, not this…"

It was the most painful thing she'd ever said to me—and on my wedding day. "I would die for you, baby. In a heartbeat."

Her eyes moved back to mine.

"And I promise I will never hurt you."

Her eyes dropped.

"Look at me."

Her eyes instantly obeyed me.

"I promise I will be faithful to you. I promise I will be honest with you. I promise I will protect you. I will be the best husband there ever was—if you give me a chance." I spoke my vows to her in that café instead of in the church, but it felt better this way, just the two of us, both broken.

Her eyes dropped to her coffee.

"I promise you."

"This is why I don't want to do this…"

I waited, hoping she would say more.

"I don't want to marry you, because…I don't want to be in that position again…where you can hurt me. I refuse to let you hurt me again. I've turned off my heart and locked it in a cage, but I'm afraid you're going to find the key and break in."

"I will find the key, baby."

She looked at me again.

"That's why I want to marry you. So I can find that key and fix what I broke."

She stared at me, eyes wet with emotion, her coffee turning cold in front of her. Her makeup had smeared when she'd taken off down the street and her hair was tangled from the cold wind, but she never looked more beautiful to me, in a wedding dress with my coat, sitting across from me in that café.

"Come on, baby." I extended my hand to her across the table. "Let's do this."

Her eyes stayed on mine before they dropped to my hand, sitting in the middle of the table for her to take. A solid minute passed, and her breathing changed, becoming deep and labored. But then she raised her hand and placed it in mine, her fingers lightly touching my skin.

Once I had her, I grabbed her.

And this time, I wouldn't let go.

I stood at the front of the church with Theo beside me, waiting for the ceremony to commence. Everyone was back in their seats, quiet now that they knew a wedding would truly take place.

The music started, and the procession began.

The bridesmaids came down the aisle, and then Scarlett's little cousins came down as the flower children. The music changed when it was time for the bride to arrive, and everyone stood up to greet her.

Dante and Scarlett appeared in the double doors, her hands gripping the white bouquet. Dante cradled her arm in his and guided her forward, the tight dress beautiful over her curves.

It was the first time I actually looked at her in her dress. She had been hidden under my coat and in too much distress for me to take in her entire appearance earlier. But now I did…and she was breathtaking.

It was a long walk down the aisle, everyone turned to face her.

She looked at the people she passed, looked at the priest at the front, and when she ran out of things to look at, she finally looked at me. When her eyes locked on mine, they stuck, the intensity in my gaze capturing her the way a predator captured its prey.

Closer and closer she came, almost within reach, almost mine.

Once she was my wife, once she carried my name, nothing would divide us again. Dante's power and influence would be limited because I would be her family, not him.

Dante stopped in front of me, kissed his daughter on the temple, and then finally gave me her hand.

I took it and squeezed it tightly, finally claiming what was mine.

I guided her next to me, in front of the priest, and took her other hand.

She'd fixed her makeup and adjusted her hair before the ceremony began. Now it looked like her escape attempt had never happened. Her cheeks had color because she was warm, and her eyes had a luminance I couldn't describe. Her touch was still hesitant, but her gaze was passionate.

The priest began the ceremony.

And I married her.

15

SCARLETT

The ballroom was lit with chandeliers, the round tables covered with champagne-gold linens and tall vases of white flowers. Friends and family were everywhere, mostly on my side since Axel's parents had chosen not to come, and therefore, his other family members chose to opt out as well.

It was a beautiful wedding, but it still didn't feel like mine.

Axel came up from behind me and took my hand. "Dance with me." He pulled me with him and didn't pause for an objection. A slow song came over the sound system for our first dance, and after he spun me around, he pulled me close, his hand in mine, and swayed from side to side with me, his big palm flat against my lower back.

His blue eyes were on me, his jawline shaved clean for the special day, and he looked at me the way he always had—like I was the only thing that mattered. "I like that dress." A faint smile moved across his lips, a playfulness entering his eyes.

It was the Axel I remembered, but he was here in the present, not in an old memory. I bowed my head and focused on his tie and his dark blue suit.

"Baby, look at me."

I lifted my gaze and looked at him again.

The playfulness was gone, replaced by that hard intensity that made him look almost angry.

"You're fucking beautiful."

My instinct was to look away, but his fingertips caught my chin and kept me still.

"Eyes on me."

At the end of the night, we left the ballroom in disarray, champagne spilled on the floor, a half-eaten wedding cake still on the stands, dirty dishes still scattered on the tables. Some people took the flowers out of the vases to enjoy them at home.

Axel and I left and stepped into the elevator to take us to the top floor.

My heart started as the size of a plum but quickly grew to a coconut. It took up all my chest, made it tight, made it hard to breathe.

Axel stood there with his hands in his pockets, looking straight ahead as the floor numbers changed on the screen. Then the doors opened, and we entered an empty hallway, taking the long walk down the maroon rug to the last door at the very end, in the corner of the building.

He slipped the keycard inside and then stepped into the room, a penthouse that had a living room with a dining table, a separate bedroom, and an enormous balcony that overlooked the private gardens of the hotel.

I could hardly breathe. My palms were covered with streaks of sweat, but my arms were pebbled with bumps from the chill. This was the moment I should be excited for, but the nerves were too much.

Axel immediately stripped off his jacket and tossed it over the armrest of the nearest couch. Then he yanked his tie free, looking out the window to the balcony as he pulled on the silk. He dropped the tie on the jacket and kept going, unbuttoning his crisp white shirt until it opened across his chest. He yanked that off too, showing his muscled back and the bulging triceps at the backs of his arms. "I hate wearing suits." He left his slacks on, low on his hips, and turned back toward me.

My eyes immediately flicked away so it wouldn't be obvious that I had stared at his perfect body with appreciation. I'd slept with him before so this shouldn't be hard, but now it felt different. He was my husband, but it felt rushed. I didn't expect to get a say in the matter.

He walked to the dresser and grabbed a leather-bound book before he moved to the dining table. "Sit down." He pulled out the chair for me at the head of the table.

I hesitated as I stared at the chair. "Why?"

"All you've eaten today is that scone. Come on, let's order something."

I'd expected him to rip off my wedding dress and throw me on the bed.

His hand rested on the back of the chair as he studied me. "We can consummate the marriage another night."

My eyes lifted to his in surprise. "I assumed that's what you wanted—"

"I do want it, but it's very clear that you don't." There was no anger or disapproval in his words. "That's not how I want our first time to be, out of obligation. So, let's have dinner. Change out of your dress."

I'd been wearing the gown all night, and it was heavy and restrictive.

He took a seat in the other chair then opened the menu, shirtless in just his slacks, the sexiest guy I'd ever seen.

But I just couldn't…not right now.

I stepped into the bedroom and shut the door before I began the painstaking task of popping all the buttons and getting out of the dress that weighed at least ten pounds. I finally got free and hung it up on the hanger, leaving it in the closet, unsure where else to put something so large.

I opened my suitcase that had been delivered and pulled out my pajamas, dark blue silk pants with a white t-shirt. I left my bra on so he wouldn't have to see my nipples through the thin fabric. When I returned to the other room, he was where I'd left him, flipping through the pages of the in-room dining menu.

I returned to the seat at the head of the table, and he slid the menu toward me.

Now that the pressure was off, my appetite roared to life. All I'd had was that single scone all day, and I hadn't eaten the day before either. How I didn't feel like I was going to pass out was a mystery to me. "What are you getting?"

"You really have to guess?" A charming smile moved to his lips. "Pizza."

I gave a slight nod before I looked at the menu again. "Of course." The memories that once brought me joy now brought me sadness.

"What about you?"

"I didn't realize how hungry I was until now."

His gaze was hot on my face. "Because you've been stressed all day."

I closed the menu. "I'm ready."

He pulled out his phone and opened the app. He handed me the phone so I could put in my order, and when I was done, I handed it back. He added his items then grinned. "So, you did get the pizza."

"It sounded good."

He continued to smile. "And fries…and a milkshake… excellent choices." He finished the order then set his phone aside. He relaxed further in the chair then crossed his leg, resting his ankle on the opposite knee.

We remained there in silence, at midnight, sitting together at the dining table instead of rolling around in the sheets.

He continued to stare at me, his blue eyes soft, taking in my features like I was a painting rather than a person.

It was hard to believe we were husband and wife, legally and spiritually bound. This was the man who'd broken my heart into so many pieces that I was certain it would never fully heal. He was the man I'd fallen for almost instantly, but I was too scared to admit that, especially to myself.

His stare continued like he could look at me forever. His arms were on the armrests, and on his left hand was the black ring he'd bought himself because he knew I wouldn't buy him one.

"You knew I'd stolen that ring…" The memory came back to me, the two of us talking in front of that painting, my heart rate slowing after I'd gotten away with the theft.

He continued his hard stare after a heavy stretch of silence. "Yes."

"You didn't say anything."

"I knew what you were doing. And I knew your father was the one who put you up to that."

"What do you mean, you knew what I was doing?"

"I knew your father was collecting the skull rings to present to Theo," he said. "To get rid of me for good."

My father's plan had been doomed from the beginning—and he'd had no idea.

"I also know you would never do something like that unless you were forced to—"

"He didn't force me—"

"Yes, he did."

"He asked me, and I said yes."

"Asking someone to do something when you know they don't want to is forcing them." His gaze turned cold. "Pretty despicable, if you ask me."

I looked away, feeling ashamed for what I'd done and also hurt that he spoke of my father that way. "This marriage isn't going to work if you insult my father like that." I looked down at the menu even though we'd already ordered, just to have something to look at.

Axel didn't say anything, but his silence was heavy.

A minute passed. Then two. I looked up once again.

His stare was cold. "He's got you pinned under his thumb, and he knows it."

"I helped him because I wanted to—"

"*Bullshit*. You helped him because you live for his validation, live for his love. Because your mother didn't want you, you feel indebted to him for raising you. You're blinded by your gratitude, but you should never have to feel grateful for someone loving you. Because if it's real, it's unconditional—"

"Didn't realize you were a licensed psychologist."

He paused, his expression angry. "If you took him out of the equation, you wouldn't be in this world. You would be a chef running a Michelin-starred restaurant. You wouldn't be stealing rings from men who could snap your neck. You know I'm right."

I turned my gaze and looked out the windows, the lamps in the room casting a gentle glow around the suite. "I meant what I said. Insult my father, and this marriage is over."

He stared at me, his fingers balling into a fist. "My job is to have your back, tell you what you *need* to hear, not what you *want* to hear. That's not going to change, and you'll be grateful for it someday. I don't like your father for a lot of reasons, but I hate him for what he's done to you."

"What has he done to me?" I snapped. "He believes I'm capable of taking his place—and that's the greatest compliment he could give me."

"No." His fingers remained tight in a fist. "He never believed that. He tried to hook you up with Theo so he could be connected to someone powerful through marriage, like this is the fifteen hundreds or something."

"That's not true—"

"Then why did he press you to date him?"

"Theo asked me out, and he just suggested it—"

"No. He told Theo he would work with him if he married you. That's what fucking happened."

I stared at him, my stomach clenching painfully. "I don't believe you."

"Then fucking ask him."

"He just wants a man who can protect me—"

"You're his fucking pawn, and you're too blind to see it—"

"Fuck you." I pushed out of the chair and stormed off, ready to leave the room and walk in the fucking cold to my father's house. I was barefoot and in my pajamas, but I didn't give a shit.

"Scarlett."

I marched to the front door and flung it open. "Fuck off, Axel."

He pushed his body against it and forced it shut, his chiseled physique like a mountain against the door. "Listen to me—"

"Move."

"I said, listen to me—"

I slapped him across the face. "Don't tell me what to do."

He moved slightly with the hit but didn't retaliate, slowly turning back to look at me again. "I'm sorry." He inhaled a slow breath, processing his annoyance. "This is not how I wanted this night to go—"

"Then don't try to poison me with lies and turn me against my father. I'm not stupid. You said you wanted to marry me, but now I wonder if this is all a scheme for revenge, to take away the one thing my father actually cares about—"

"I married you because I wanted to." His eyes bored into mine, beautiful and angry at the same time, his back still against the door. "I married you because I want to be with you, because I fucking miss you, because these last six months have been shit without you. And I know you believe me when I say that."

I was so angry, I wanted to keep arguing, but when he spoke like that and looked like that as he said all those things, I was stunned into silence. My chin dropped, and I stared at his chest instead of him.

"The last thing I want to do is push you away."

My eyes stayed down.

"Baby, come back to me."

Why did I feel warm at the sound of his voice? Why did I get weak when he gazed at me like that? Why did I lift my chin and look up at him when I shouldn't want to look at him ever again?

"I'm sorry," he repeated. "Forget what I said."

"So, you are lying—"

"I'm not lying," he snapped. "But *this* is more important than being right."

My chin dropped again, knowing I should hate him for all the shit he'd said but physically unable to.

His fingers moved underneath my chin and lifted my head.

I didn't fight it, feeling a surge of heat at his touch.

He stared at me, his face just inches from mine, his blue eyes focused hard on my features.

My breaths quickened and deepened, the intensity so heavy it was painful. He was so close to me, so close that he could kiss me, and judging by the look on his face, he wanted to.

He glanced at my lips then looked at me again.

I inhaled an unnecessary breath.

He withdrew his touch and stepped back from me. "The food will be here soon." He returned my chair to the table then left it pulled out for me to sit.

I stared at the chair for a moment before I sat down, feeling the seat cushioning my ass as I dropped down. When his hand left the back of the chair, it grazed my hair, catching a couple strands before he returned to his seat and resumed his heated stare.

We ate in silence, each of us having our own pizza and sharing the fries that I'd ordered. He'd also gotten a bottle of wine for us to share.

It was two in the morning now, and while I was exhausted, my hunger was far more potent.

He didn't eat nearly as much as I did, focusing on his wine more than anything else.

I ate almost my entire pizza, most of the fries, and even downed the shake by myself.

He wore a look of amusement, like the sight was entertaining for him.

"I was starving."

"I could tell," he said with a slight smile, his hands together as his elbows remained propped on the armrests.

I glanced at the bedroom, wondering if he would sleep in the bed with me. I was so tired, I almost didn't care where he slept. "Will you sleep on the couch?"

"No."

"You expect me to sleep on the couch?"

He smirked like I'd made a joke. "No."

"I told you I wanted to sleep in different bedrooms—"

"It's our wedding night."

"What happened to not forcing someone to do what they don't want to do?"

His smile slowly disappeared. "I'm your husband—"

"I don't want to sleep with you."

"Why?"

"Because I don't."

He paused for a moment. "Tell me why."

I looked away.

"Baby."

"I told you to stop calling me that."

"It's hard not to," he said quietly. "Because when I look at you…I see my baby. Now tell me why."

My eyes remained averted. "Because stuff will happen…"

"I would never pressure you into something you don't want to do, as I've proven."

I swallowed before I answered. "That's not what I'm worried about." I didn't want to see the smirk on his face. Didn't want to see the victory in his eyes. He wasn't the problem, but I was.

There was no smile in his voice. "There's nothing wrong with wanting me."

"I disagree."

"I'm your husband—"

"And the man who has broken me beyond all repair." I'd spent those six months trying to convince myself I was okay, when I was anything but. "For the first month, all I did was stay home every night and cry. There were days when I couldn't get out of bed, so I lied and said I was sick, when my father knew I wasn't. Then I started to drink a lot, going through a bottle of wine by myself every night. When that didn't work, I turned to sex. But that just made me feel lonelier." I could feel his stare on the side of my face even though I couldn't see him. It was like a spot of sunlight on a summer day. "And when that didn't work, I came to the conclusion that nothing would ever work. So I've been walking this world like a zombie, feeling nothing at all." The silence stretched after I finished speaking.

Axel didn't say anything. What could he possibly say to that?

After a moment of silence, I turned back to look at him.

His face was flushed, his veins were more prominent, and his eyes were on the table in silent rage.

I wasn't sure if he was mad at me for saying that—or mad at himself for causing that despair. "I know our relationship was brief, just a couple months, but…you really meant a lot to me."

His voice escaped as a whisper. "I know, baby."

I looked at the bedroom behind him then rose from my chair. It was late, and I was ready for bed, ready for this conversation to end. I walked away, and he didn't try to stop me.

"I just wish you knew how much you meant to me."

The next day, we left the hotel and returned to his apartment, my new home.

My bedroom was on the same floor, down the hallway in a suite that was much smaller than his. A four-poster bed was in the middle of the room, with two nightstands and a dresser. There was a large TV on the wall, and then on the side of the room was a desk that faced the balcony doors. It had its own bathroom, so I didn't have to walk down the hallway.

All the boxes of my stuff had been delivered, my clothes and shoes, my keepsakes. I'd left all my furniture behind and had decided to rent the apartment out for extra income. Axel and I hadn't discussed finances, but I assumed he would have his money and I would have mine. Nothing would change on that front.

"What do you think?" Axel appeared in the doorway.

"It's nice." I looked at all the boxes, all the stuff I had to go through. "Am I free to use the kitchen?"

"You're free to use anything you want," he said. "This place is yours as much as it's mine."

I felt like a visitor—a permanent one.

"The chef will make you anything you want. Just ask."

"But I like to cook." I turned to look at him, seeing him in dark jeans and a t-shirt, just as handsome as he'd been in his suit on our wedding day.

"There are two kitchens in the house. Use the other one whenever you wish."

"Why do you have two kitchens?"

"One is for cooking, and one is for entertaining."

"Do you entertain a lot?"

He shook his head. "Not like I used to." His eyes scanned the boxes stacked on the floor. "Need help?"

"No, it's okay."

"I have plenty of space for you in my suite."

I looked away. "I'm fine."

There was a long pause before he responded. "Alright." His footsteps sounded then disappeared.

I looked at all the stuff I had to unpack, all the boxes of my belongings, all the things that gave me my identity. My wedding dress was the only thing hung up in the closet at the moment.

I gave a sigh before I got to work.

I was alone in my room when he texted me. *Have dinner with me.*

I didn't text him back, choosing to ignore him rather than say no.

I'm not asking, baby.

You're forcing me to do something I don't want to do. I threw his words back at him, the best excuse to get out of his company.

You agreed to marry me, not be roommates. Your bedroom is for sleeping only. I expect you to spend the rest of your time with me. If that's a problem, then I'll come and get you. I'll give you five minutes.

I sighed as I read his message.

And I'm not forcing you—as you admitted last night.

This was just the first day of this arrangement, of this long-term plan to backstab Axel the way he'd backstabbed me, but it was already challenging. I was used to living alone, and now I had a husband whom I had feelings for…whom I couldn't trust.

I went down the hallway to his bedroom and let myself inside.

He was on the couch in just his sweatpants and nothing else, his chest hard as though carved with a razor-sharp knife. A game was on the TV, and the bottle of scotch was on the table, the room looking like a bachelor pad.

He immediately turned his head to look at me. "Good choice."

It was the first time I'd been in his bedroom since he'd dumped me. I remembered climbing onto his lap on that very couch, hoping the feeling of our bodies together would fix all our problems.

I looked away when the memory became too much. I'd ridden him bareback, and I wondered if he'd already fucked Cassandra prior to that. It was good luck I didn't catch anything.

I moved to the armchair on the other side of the living room, sitting as far away as I possibly could.

Axel gave a quiet sigh, like he knew the exact thoughts that crossed my mind. "Is there something you'd like to watch?"

"The game is fine." I grabbed a blanket from the basket and pulled it over me.

Instead of looking at the TV, he looked at me. His black wedding ring contrasted against the fair skin on his left hand.

I only wore my wedding ring outside the house, so I'd left it on my nightstand in the bedroom.

He continued to stare at me.

"What?" I asked without looking at him.

"It's hard to be patient when I want you so much."

My eyes remained focused on the screen, careful not to react, not to swallow.

"Just to hold you…"

I did my best to ignore him, my broken heart in pieces on the floor. Where I should feel nothing but hate and resentment, I felt warmth. I craved his touch as much as I always had, and I hated myself for being so weak. I'd never thought I would be one of those women who went back to a cheating ex, but here I was, falling under his spell. I was too proud to let that show. "When's dinner?"

A long stretch of silence passed, like my question had struck him as an insult.

The butler knocked on the door minutes later then delivered our dinner on a cart. There had to be a service elevator somewhere in the apartment for him to get up here with the food. He set up the dining table with our dinner, placing a basket of fresh bread in the center along with our salads and entrées.

He poured two glasses of wine then left.

Axel turned off the TV and walked to the dining table, taking a seat without waiting for me.

I joined him a moment later, taking the seat across from him.

He had grilled chicken with a side of greens, but my dinner had mashed potatoes and gravy.

He cut into his meat and ate as he watched me.

"It's good," I said, sliding my fork through the potatoes.

"Not as good as yours."

"That's not true."

"I wish you were my chef, but I'd rather have you as my wife." He took another bite and chewed, watching me from across the table.

No one ever stared at me as much as he did. Most men couldn't hold eye contact that long, but Axel by far was the most confident man I'd ever been with. He made me nervous every time he stared, not because I was afraid, but because of the way it made me burn.

The meal was spent in silence.

He continued to stare but didn't engage me in conversation.

I grabbed a piece of bread and smeared it with butter before I took a bite.

His stare remained.

"You didn't mention you had a brother."

He continued to chew his bite.

"And he looks nothing like you." They were both exceptionally sexy men, but their appearances couldn't be more different.

"He's not my biological brother."

"Then he's adopted?"

He shook his head.

"So, he's not your brother at all?"

"He's more my family than my own parents are." He ate much quicker than I did, so his plate was already wiped clean. But he sat there and drank his wine as he waited for me to finish before leaving the table.

"How long have you known him?"

"A long time," he said. "He's the one who got me out of prison."

"So, he believed you?"

"Of course he did." That endless stare resumed. "Just like you."

When the stare became too much, I dropped my eyes back to my plate. Being alone with him was different in his bedroom. All the memories of the fucking and soaking we did in his tub pressed up against me hard, made me hot under the collar. "Have you ever considered giving her money to tell your parents the truth?"

"That would mean she'd have to incriminate herself, and I could get her on criminal charges. I wouldn't do that, but I could."

"You wouldn't?"

He gave a slight shake of his head. "It's done. Whether she pays me money or goes to jail, it doesn't change what I've already lost."

"Maybe if you promised her you wouldn't retaliate, she could tell your parents—"

"I really don't think it'd make a difference anyway," he said. "My parents despise me."

"That's not true—"

"Trust me, it is." He crossed his arms over his chest, his eyes on his glass, his stare angry.

"I—I just don't know how a parent could hate their kid so much, even if you were guilty of the crime. People change, and they should have given you the chance to reform."

"And maybe that would have eventually occurred... someday, but more things have happened, and now there's no chance for a reconciliation."

"Like what?" I asked, only interested in him and not my dinner.

He turned to look out the window, giving a loud sigh as he considered his forthcoming words. "Someone in the game captured my father and threatened to kill him if I didn't meet their demands. As much as I didn't want to give them what they wanted..." His eyes remained fixated on the window. "I didn't have a choice. I folded to save my father's life. But of course, the asshole shot him anyway."

"Oh my god." I dropped my fork. "Is he okay?"

"The bullet shattered the bone in his arm, and it's taken five surgeries to fix it. He'll be in pain for the rest of his life."

"Jesus…" I felt like shit as I stared at the side of his face.

"That was the nail in the coffin." He looked at me again. "No coming back from that."

"I'm so sorry." If someone had done that to my father, I would be beside myself. It would haunt me forever.

His blue eyes looked at mine, devoid of emotion. "It's not your fault."

"Did you kill the guy who did this to you?"

He inhaled a slow breath. "No."

"Why?" I snapped.

"Because I can't," he said. "It's complicated." He looked out the window again, relaxed in the chair, his body massive with all those muscles on top of muscles. "Theo is one of the only people who's always had my back. I have other guys who mean a lot to me, but it's different with him. We both come from broken families, so we made a family with each other."

"That's sweet." I thought about my date with Theo, every interaction that seemed off. "Now I understand why he acted like that." I smirked because it was a little embarrassing that I'd thrown myself at him and he knew he couldn't act on it.

"Acted like what?"

I wasn't sure if I should tell him, but I suspected Theo had probably already mentioned it. "I kinda came on to him a couple times, but he never took the bait."

His expression remained the same, but his eyes were a little harsh.

"At the time, it didn't make sense. Why ask me on a date if you don't want to seal the deal after dinner? But now I realize he was never going to cross that line because of you." I had been disappointed that Theo wouldn't put out, and his rejection had made me question my appeal. Now I felt better knowing it had nothing to do with me at all.

Axel remained quiet, his eyes shifting back to the window.

"You're angry."

He spoke with a quiet voice. "I'm not angry."

"Nothing happened—"

"I'm not angry about that." He turned back to me. "Why would Theo ask you out if he couldn't act on it?"

I stared back at him.

"Doesn't make sense, right?"

My heart started to clench.

"Just something to think about."

16

AXEL

I walked into the back room of the strip club and found Theo in one of the armchairs, talking to one of his guys while his eyes watched the brunette spin around the pole in front of him. The cigar rested between his fingertips before he brought it to his lips.

"You lied to me." I smacked it out of his hand then watched it fly across the room. "Fucking asshole."

All of his guys pulled out their guns.

Theo was visibly stunned, but he raised his hand then lowered it to tell the guys to lower their guns. Then he got to his feet and stared me dead in the eyes, the music still playing, the girls still dancing, probably because they were used to this sort of thing. "Lied about what?"

"You said nothing happened."

It took a second for him to understand the accusation. "Because nothing did happen, Axel."

"So you're saying my wife didn't try to fuck you?" I snapped. "Because that fucking sounds like something."

Theo looked at his guys and lowered his hand again, getting them to stand down. "Come on, let's talk." He led the way out of the private room and into the main portion of the strip club. He walked outside, heading to the front of the unremarkable building that hid the truth of its contents with its lack of signage. It was quiet except for the sounds of cars and motorbikes that passed on the street.

I rounded on him right away. "What the fuck, Theo?"

"Why did she even tell you that?"

"Because she said everything made much more sense after she realized how close we are. I asked her to elaborate."

"You shouldn't have asked her—"

"You shouldn't have lied to me," I snapped, wanting to shove him in the chest.

"Would you rather me tell you she wanted to fuck?" he asked incredulously. "You want me to hurt you?"

My hands moved to my hips, unsure what to do, how to take out my anger. "I want to know exactly what happened."

"Why?"

"Because I do—"

"Why?" he repeated. "It's just going to make you feel like shit."

"Did she have feelings for you?"

"No," he said without hesitation. "In fact, I asked her out again, and she said she was only interested in hooking up, so if I wasn't interested in that, I should leave her alone. She may have wanted me for the night, but we both know it's because she couldn't have the man she really wants. So calm the fuck down."

My hands cupped my face, and then I slowly dragged them down as I gave a growl.

"Nothing. Happened." He stared at me. "You know she's been with other people, so why does this bother you so much?"

My arms crossed over my chest, and I stared at the ground. "Because you aren't other people, Theo. If you guys hooked up, something could have happened, and then she'd be married to you instead of me."

His stare continued before the ferocity faded. "You know I'm not interested in anything serious, so that wouldn't have happened."

"She would have changed your mind. Trust me on that."

"But it didn't happen," Theo said. "We're speaking in hypotheticals here, which is stupid."

"If you hadn't said no—"

"But I did say no," he barked. "Because I would never cross that line. I know what she means to you."

I felt like shit for a lot of reasons. Theo was a really good-looking guy, and knowing Scarlett was attracted to him made me jealous to no end. And if he had slept with her and then they'd gotten together, I never would have gotten her back—all because of Dante. "If you weren't loyal to me, Dante would have completely ruined my life."

He continued to watch me, both of us standing in the cold in t-shirts without being affected by the weather.

"She's a beautiful woman, and so spicy she makes me sweat, but there was something off with her. Like only half of her was present with me, and the other half was hidden in a vault. Maybe she wanted me for the night, but I can tell you're the man she wants for the rest of her life."

I gave a quiet sigh. "I don't know about that."

"Be patient, man."

"Getting her close to me is like pulling fucking teeth."

"You knew it would be this way when you asked her to marry you."

"It still fucking sucks," I snapped. "There are moments when I know she's still there…she's still with me, but then she gets scared and closes me off again. It's a step forward and three steps back."

"Did you tell her that Dante wanted me to marry her?"

"Yes."

"And her response?"

"She didn't believe me, and it turned into a big fight."

"She's a beautiful woman. Why would I turn down her offer to fuck—"

My eyes were like a knife across his face.

He corrected himself. "It doesn't make sense, is all I'm saying. My behavior supports your accusation. She must realize that."

"I think she does, but she refuses to let herself believe it. It's a compartment inside another compartment. She's so fucking brainwashed by this guy, and she doesn't even see it. It's so damn infuriating." I threw my arms down. "I'm the one person she can trust, but she trusts me the least."

When I got home, I knocked on her bedroom door, and there was no answer. I let myself inside and saw she was nowhere around. I headed downstairs and checked the study, wondering if she'd decided to claim that room as hers, but she wasn't there either. I asked my butler about it. "When was the last time you saw Scarlett?"

"Mrs. Moreau left the property four hours ago."

"Did she say where she was headed?"

"No," he said. "But she and I exchange very few words…"

She doesn't say much to me either. "Thank you, Aldo." I stepped away and texted her. *Where are you?*

At work.

Aldo said you left the house four hours ago.

Yes. And now I'm at work.

You mean you're at your father's house.

Yes.

That's not the office anymore.

I'm busy, Axel. We'll talk later.

Maybe I should just kill Dante. My wife already hated me enough as it was.

I headed to his estate, passed through the gates and parked next to my wife's cheap car. I insisted she drive one of my nicer rides, but she refused. She was married to me on paper, but not emotionally, physically, or financially.

I walked up to the doors and let myself inside, knowing both Dante and Scarlett were aware I was there the second I stepped onto the premises.

She was in the parlor, working at one of the tables in a pencil skirt and blouse, looking like a sexy secretary that I should bend over my desk. Our wedding had been a week ago, and I hadn't even hugged her, let alone fucked her.

She looked up when I entered, and as if we were back in time, when I flirted with her left and right to get her attention, we were back to a heated but distant liaison.

The most difficult part of our relationship was the fact that I knew she wanted me, had listened to her admit it, but she refused to act on it. She wouldn't sleep with me for fear of opening her legs. She wouldn't allow herself to be vulnerable with me whatsoever. I knew I had to be patient because she would break at some point, and once that happened…I would get my chance to win back her heart.

She looked back at her computer and ignored me.

That made me snap her laptop closed. "That was rude."

"Really?" she asked. "Because showing up here isn't rude?"

"You're my wife. I can show up wherever you are whenever I feel like it." I pulled the laptop to my side of the table so she wouldn't try to open it again. "I made it clear that you would work from home—*our home*."

"I'm used to working here—"

"I don't care. My bottom line is none of your father's business. He gets his cut, and that's it."

She was still as she stared at me, her eyes burning in their anger. "I want to spend time with him—"

"Then go out to dinner with him. See a movie. I don't care. I want you at home."

"Don't tell me what to do—"

"I will tell you what the fuck to do when it comes to my business."

"It's half mine, asshole."

I slid the laptop back at her and got to my feet. "We made a deal. A marriage for a business. I feel like I'm not getting my end of the deal here because you haven't made even the smallest effort to participate." My patience had run so thin that it barely held on. "So maybe we should just get an annulment and go our separate ways because I'm tired of this bullshit." I marched off and headed to the door.

"Axel."

I ignored her, stormed out to the car, and took off.

I sat on the couch in my room, drinking my scotch and watching the game, pissed off with no release. I had dinner alone and didn't bother to wait for her. She was probably in her bedroom down the hall, and I wouldn't see her until tomorrow, if I saw her at all.

A knock sounded on my door.

"What?" I barked, knowing I shouldn't talk to Aldo like that if it was him.

But it was Scarlett, my loving wife.

I gave her a cold stare before I looked at the TV again. "What?" I repeated, angrier than before.

She was still in the clothes she'd worn earlier, like she'd stayed there after I stormed off. In her pumps, she joined me in the living room and sat in the armchair close by. It was the closest she'd come to me voluntarily. "I thought about what you said…and you're right."

"Yeah?" I asked, letting my attitude come through, the frustration unrestrained. I took a drink and looked at the TV.

"Axel."

I ignored her.

"Please look at me."

I set my glass down and looked directly at her, her eyes beautiful with the dark shadow across the lids, her lips a pretty pink from her gloss, her hair in soft curls that I wanted to fist.

"I'm sorry I've been so distant. I've just…been having a hard time with this." Her eyes shifted away like it was too hard to look at me. "But you're right. You asked for a marriage, and I haven't given that to you."

I couldn't believe she'd said any of that. I half expected her to ask for a divorce and back out of the arrangement.

"I'm sorry," she said. "It's just hard."

All my anger disappeared at seeing her being vulnerable with me for the first time. She was close, close enough that I could grab her hand if I wanted to. "I promised I wouldn't hurt you. But I can't fulfill that promise if you won't let me."

She looked down at her hands. "I know." She continued to keep her eyes down. "If this were just an arranged marriage and we had no history, it would be different. I'd be married to a sexy man and it would be fun, but that's not how it is." Her eyes finally lifted to mine, guarded but still vulnerable. "I've never stopped caring about you, not even after what you did."

My heart gave a twinge of pain because it was so fucking hard to sit there and listen to her tell me how much I'd crushed her, over and over, and be powerless to speak the truth. To tell her how I really felt.

"I—I just can't go through that again."

I left the couch and moved to my knee in front of her, our eyes still level. My hand grabbed hers, and I placed it over my heart, right against my hot skin, my other hand cradling her arm in my grasp. "You won't."

Her eyes softened, and that heavy guard started to dissolve.

I said the words like they were vows. "I promise you won't."

17

SCARLETT

The study downstairs was huge, a large mahogany desk on a rug, a grand fireplace that took up most of the wall. Two couches faced each other with a glass table in the middle, and the other side of the room was windows and curtains.

I preferred the mahogany desk to the little desk in my bedroom and used it instead. As far as I could tell, it seemed like Axel hardly used this room. I'd never even seen him on a laptop before. Wasn't sure if he had one. He owned this large villa but only used the fraction of it in his bedroom.

The doors to the study were open, so Axel walked inside, wearing dark jeans, a long-sleeved shirt, and boots. He entered the room, tall and muscular, and dropped into one of the armchairs in front of the desk. "What do you think?"

"About?"

"The study." He crossed his ankle on the opposite knee and propped his elbow on one of the armrests.

"It's nice. Really nice."

"You can have it. I never use it."

"Where do you do your paperwork?"

"On the couch in front of the TV."

"I've never seen you work."

"Because I don't give a shit about work when you're in the room." He rested his chin on his closed knuckles and stared at me across the big desk.

His blue eyes were possessive, like he wanted to reach across that big slab of wood and grab me. I took in his stare and then severed the contact when I looked at my laptop. "I think I finished the numbers for the week. Things are looking good."

"That's what I hear."

"My father is trying to resolve the production issues."

"I'm sure he'll figure it out." He continued to stare at me the same way, touching me from clear across the room. "I have a dinner party tonight. I'd like you to come with me."

"A dinner party?"

"A diplomat from the US."

"And why are you having dinner with him?"

"Connections."

"We barely have enough product to meet our demand."

"But once your father figures it out, we'll have another revenue stream."

"I'm all for making money, but we don't want to grow too much, too fast."

"These things take time," he said. "I'll just have a couple drinks with him and compliment his wife. Pretty simple."

"Then what do you need me for?"

His stare hardened. "Because you're my wife—and you go where I go."

I wore a black dress with hints of gold, held up by a single strap across one shoulder, tight over my stomach and hips. I paired it with gold heels and a gold bracelet. My wedding ring clashed because it was platinum, but I couldn't go out without wearing it.

Axel arrived at my bedroom door and knocked.

I grabbed my clutch and slid my phone inside before I stepped into the hallway.

He was in black jeans and dress boots, wearing a dark blue button-up that was open at the top, revealing a spot of his chest. He looked me over, his warm eyes showing how pleased he was by my appearance. He complimented me with just a stare. "I like that dress."

Memories rushed back to me, all the times he would say those words with a sly grin. "Thanks."

We walked together down the stairs then took the elevator to the garage. That time was spent in silence, the tension locked in the elevator with us as we moved underground. When the doors opened, some of that discomfort floated out, but it was still trapped around our bodies.

He picked one of his cars, and we drove onto the street, the engine roaring every time he hit the gas with his heavy foot. One time we were in the car together, he'd grabbed my hand and held it in my lap. I'd swooned on the spot. But he didn't do that this time—and I wasn't sure if I would have let him anyway.

He drove across town, close to where my old apartment was, and then pulled past the gates to the property. We parked our car then headed to the double doors hugged by two enormous pots that held olive trees.

Halfway there, his arm hooked around my waist, and he brought me a little closer.

That was all it took to make me feel it, the spark that used to ignite me into an inferno. Any time he touched me, I felt that same potent longing, that same desperation that had driven me into his arms night after night.

He knocked on the door, and then the butler greeted us. He took my coat and hung it on the rack before he guided us into the parlor, where everyone was having a drink while appetizers were passed around.

I felt a wave of nervousness when I looked at the room full of people I didn't know. Making small talk with strangers that I would never see again felt exhausting, but to support Axel...my husband...I'd have to put on a good face.

"Alexander, it's nice to see you." He must be the diplomat because he spoke English with an American accent. He greeted Axel with a handshake then turned to me. "And this lovely lady?"

"This is my wife, Scarlett." The pride was noticeable in his voice. "We just got married a couple weeks ago."

"Oh, newlyweds." He shook my hand. "I'm surprised you found the time to get away and be here."

"Wouldn't miss it," Axel said. "I know you aren't in town often."

The butler got me a drink, and I mingled with the socialites I didn't know. Some of them worked in government, and some of them were from the UK. It still shocked me how much government and criminality went together, like the perfect pairing of wine and cheese.

Axel kept his arm around my waist and hugged me close, his fingers gripping me tighter than necessary, like I would slip out of his grasp and disappear. When the appetizers were finished, we sat down to dinner, and Axel spoke to the diplomat about politics—

politics outside of Italy, in places like the UK and France and even the United States. He was well-informed on international news, like he read multiple newspapers every single morning.

When dinner was finished and the plates were cleared away, Axel's hand moved to my thigh.

He didn't even seem to notice what he did because he did it in mid-sentence. His fingers dipped into the crease between my crossed thighs, his fingers just underneath the edge of my dress. His hand was warm and comfortable against my skin, but it made my heart race in a panic. It excited me but also scared me.

I was scared of how much I liked it.

How could I crave the touch of someone who hurt me so much?

When the night was over, we got into his car and headed home. It was late, almost eleven, so the streets were empty. Casually, like he did it without a second thought, he moved his hand over the center console and rested it on my thigh, returning it to the same place it'd been after dinner. His fingers were warm like the sun, and his fingers rose up my dress like he wanted to cup my thigh in the perfect spot.

My heart did all sorts of things, somersaults and spins, but also tried to run away.

With one hand on the wheel, he drove home through the quiet streets back to his villa. Well, *our* villa. The engine roared every time he hit the gas after a red light, the illumination from the dashboard highlighting his handsome face and casting shadows underneath his hard jawline. But when the light hit his blue eyes, that was really something.

He pulled into the garage then we got into the elevator.

Just as casually as he did in the car, he grabbed my hand and held it as we rose to the entryway. He stood close to me, eyes on the screen, pretending this was normal when it was the most affection we'd ever shown.

The doors opened, and we entered the quiet house. Up the stairs we went, my hand still gripped by his. My heels turned muffled once we hit the carpeted hallway. Instead of moving to the end where his bedroom was located, he stopped in front of my bedroom to drop me off.

He looked at me.

I could feel it. I could feel everything.

It was just a stare, but it contained so much more. Passion. Desire. Desperation. Without saying a word, he told me what was coming, and if I didn't want it, now was the time to speak up.

I tried to put up my walls and block him out, but I couldn't. My body couldn't do it anymore. My mind and heart had been at odds with each other for so long, but living with this man every day had weakened my resolve. I knew what he'd done was wrong, but when I looked into those beautiful blues, I saw more than his transgression. I saw a man who was kind and honest, a man who would keep his word—even though he'd already broken it.

He moved forward, making me step back into the closed door. He came closer until we were just inches apart, his face above mine, his sleeves pushed up to his elbows because he was somehow hot on a winter night.

He slid one of his muscular arms around the small of my back and got a grip so tight that I couldn't flee. He would normally grab my ass at this point, but he kept his hand in a respectful area. He dove his other hand into my hair, pushed it from my face, got it tangled in his fingertips because he dug so deep.

My fingers gripped his wrist at my neck, and I stopped breathing.

He forced my chin up, forced my stare to lock on his. Then he glanced at my lips, drew in a slow breath as he admired them. "Baby, I missed you."

The words were out of my mouth on their own, my heart betraying my mind. "I missed you too—"

His lips took mine in a swift defeat. It was a soft landing but packed with the kind of passion that made his fingers grip my hair tighter, pulling at the scalp slightly. He tightened his arm around my waist, lifting me to him slightly, forcing me to rise on my tiptoes even though I was already in heels. The kiss was soft and delicate, his lips handling mine like they were fragile pieces of glass. But then his mouth turned aggressive, taking my lips with ownership as he pressed me into the door.

I was swept away instantly, all logical thought extinguished as one arm circled his neck, while the other cupped his face. My fingers could feel the coarse stubble along his jawline, feel the hardness in his bones that contrasted with the softness of his lips.

"Fuck..." My memory wasn't an exaggeration. It was real. His kiss, his touch, it was as good as I remembered.

The kiss continued against the door, my hand gliding down to his chest to feel its hardness, to his muscular biceps to feel them too. He wore the same cologne as before, and the smell mixed with the memory of his sweat elicited even deeper memories.

And then those sexy memories changed into the last one I had of him, when he'd walked into that restaurant with Cassandra after dumping me. The moment was shattered instantly, and my lips broke apart as if his mouth had stung me like a wasp.

He let me pull away. Didn't try to kiss me again. "Stay with me." His eyes locked on mine, his hand still deep in my hair. "Baby, look at me." His hand left my back and placed my hand on his chest. "Stay with me..."

"I—I just remembered—"

"I know. Stay with me." His thumb rested in the corner of my mouth. "Live in the moment with me. Forget the past."

"How can I forget the past if you've never even apologized for it." There had never been a moment when he'd told me he'd made a horrible mistake, that he'd fucked up so bad and he wished he could take it back. Not once did that happen. He said he was sorry that I was hurt, but that was it.

His eyes shifted back and forth between mine.

"I'm ashamed to admit this, but I fantasized about you coming back to me…telling me how sorry you are…that the whole thing made you realize what you lost. But that day never came, and if it had, I'm not sure if I would have been strong enough to turn you down."

His eyes remained hard on my face, but he didn't say anything.

"You aren't going to apologize."

After a long pause, he spoke. "No."

"Why?"

"I do feel terrible every time you tell me how much you're hurting, when you tell me about the nights you cried…and the way my absence devastated you. It hurts me more than you know. It makes me angrier than you could ever fathom."

"Then why can't you apologize?"

His eyes flicked away for the first time, and he gave a sigh. "I hope one day I can tell you."

"Why can't you tell me—"

"You trusted me when most people didn't—because you knew me. I know this is a lot to ask, more than I should, but I'd like you to trust me again. Let the past go and live in this moment with me." His thumb swiped at my cheek. "Please."

My eyes dropped down to his chest, some of the skin visible because his shirt was partially open. I focused on that, feeling his hot stare on my face. I didn't have a clue why I was so weak for this man, how he could make me fall when I had every reason not to. "I'll try."

His hand left my face, and his arms moved around me, cocooning me in a hard hug. His chin rested on my head, and he squeezed me tight, holding me close to the door in the hallway, his body like living concrete.

I closed my eyes as I turned into his chest, letting my cheek rest against his hardness, feeling him breathe. It reminded me of our sleepovers, the way he held me all night, his fingers grazing my flesh.

"Thank you, baby." He released a sigh as he continued to hold me, content with having me in his arms. "Sleep with me."

A hug in the hallway felt safe, where clothes wouldn't drop. But in a bed in the darkness…that was different. Even if he lay there and didn't try anything, I would try something. There was no way I could lie beside this sexy man and keep my hands to myself. "I can't."

"I just want to sleep with you." He continued to rest his chin on the top of my head. "I promise."

"I don't think I can lie in a bed with you and…just sleep." It'd been a while since I'd had a satisfying night with a partner. The guys I'd been with couldn't hold a candle to Axel. That was why I'd been so forward with Theo, because I'd believed he was capable of doing what others couldn't.

"Nothing will happen. I promise." He pulled away so he could look at me. "Come on." His hand found mine, and he gripped it as he started to guide me down the hallway to his bedroom.

I let him pull me, comforted by his promise but also disappointed by it.

We entered his suite, a few lamps on for visibility, and he guided me into his bedroom.

I hadn't slept in that bed for more than six months, but I remembered everything about it, the firmness of the mattress, the softness of the sheets, the way they smelled like him with a hint of detergent. They were so crisp, like his housekeeper ironed them once they came out of the dryer.

Axel immediately undressed, popping open all the buttons until he removed the shirt and left it on the floor. He was facing away from me, so I could see all the muscles of his back, the way they padded his spine with strength. Then he loosened his belt and the button of his jeans before he kicked off his boots. Everything came off piece by piece, until he stood there in only his boxers.

Oh Jesus...

He ran his fingers through his short hair before he turned to me.

Was he more muscular than he used to be?

He moved to the bed and got underneath the sheets, leaving them at his waist. Then he reached up and turned off his bedside lamp. His butler had completed the turn-down service, placing a glass of water on each nightstand, like Axel had planned this before we left for dinner.

His head was propped up on his arm. "Help yourself to the dresser."

I forced my eyes away and looked at the dresser against the wall. I walked toward it, opened a drawer, and found a black t-shirt that I could wear. My heart was like a racehorse inside my chest—and I'd put all my money on him.

I considered walking into the bathroom to change, but he'd already seen me naked many times. The vanity seemed unnecessary. I turned away and unzipped my dress so it fell off. I didn't wear a bra, just tape over my nipples, so I ripped those off then pulled the shirt over my head, which fit like a soft blanket. My heels remained, so I slipped them off with my fingers then let my bare feet touch the hardwood. He got a view of my ass in my black thong, and I was certain he had stared.

I turned around and saw his face.

It was a little harder than it'd been a second ago.

I approached the bed and flicked the covers back so I could slide inside.

I slipped between the sheets and immediately smelled his scent of scotch and sandalwood and cigars.

The second my head hit the pillow, he was all over me, his strong arms dragging me across the bed until I was nestled into his side. He maneuvered me slightly on top of him, my leg crossed over his stomach, his big hand cupping my thigh.

He kissed my temple as his other hand moved underneath my shirt, touching the bare skin of my back. Then he lay still, his eyes closed, his breaths deep and even.

I lay there in the crook of his arm, my hand stretching across his hard stomach, warm in his embrace, safe in his touch. He was drop-dead gorgeous, with all those muscles and power, eyes so blue they looked like paradise, but now that I was beside him, what I wanted most was…this.

Just to be with him.

I spent the day working in the study, and once I was done for the day, I headed back to my bedroom to change for the evening. My father had asked me to dinner, and we were going to my favorite restaurant for a night packed with wine and carbs. After I changed in my bedroom, I knocked on Axel's door.

"Come in."

I walked inside and stilled when I saw him, standing there in workout shorts, drenched in sweat from head to toe. His skin glistened in the light, tinted red from all the blood flooding his muscles.

He had a container in his hand, some kind of protein mix, and he shook it before he took a drink. "Don't knock."

I missed what he said because I stared at him so hard, completely captivated by how strong and sexy this man was. Not just any man…but my husband. "Sorry?"

After he took another drink, he smirked, like he was fully aware of my distraction. "You don't need to knock. Just walk in."

"I didn't want to be rude."

"It's your house, baby. You aren't rude." He finished off his drink then left it on the table for the butler to take care of. "I'm going to hop in the shower."

Can I watch? "I'm going out to dinner with my father."

He didn't seem annoyed by that information. "Have a good time. I'll be here when you get back."

"Alright."

He walked into the bedroom then turned the corner and disappeared.

I inhaled a slow breath, suddenly hot under the collar, and then walked out.

Father and I made small talk over dinner.

I had the Bolognese pappardelle, and he had a salad—as always. Didn't even use dressing, just a squeeze of lemon. He was considering taking a trip somewhere tropical just to get away from the winter.

I hated winter, but I didn't hate this winter as much as I'd thought I would.

"How are things with Axel?" My father's eyes were down when he asked the question, as if he only asked because he felt obligated.

I knew my father didn't want the details of our marriage, how we'd just slept in the same bed for the first time last night. We'd shared our first kiss too, pressed up against the door, Axel's big hands all over me. "Good."

"He's treating you well?"

"He's always been good to me." He'd betrayed me, but everything before and after had been pleasant. The wedding ring he gave me was on my left hand, an enormous rock that I still hadn't gotten used to.

"Good." My father took a bite then lifted his gaze. "I have a couple ideas to get out of this mess."

"What mess?" I asked as I took a sip of wine.

He stopped everything he was doing to stare at me. "This arrangement with Theo and Axel."

Life had gone on since the business changed hands, and it didn't feel that much different than it did before. With the increased revenue, my father made the same as he did when he ran the company alone, so not much had changed. "Yes, of course."

"Theo mentioned possible distribution to France. My contacts tell me the kingpin who's taken over for Bartholomew is not someone to be trifled with. If I pressure Theo to take the French distribution, perhaps he'll be eliminated by this new foe. Axel, too."

"What's his name?"

"Beau."

"What do you know about him?"

"Not much," he said. "But perhaps we can come to an arrangement. I could offer him a portion of the business if he eliminates Theo and Axel. Wouldn't have to get my hands dirty at all. They wouldn't know what hit them."

"What do you mean, eliminate Theo and Axel?" I held my fork in my hand and ignored the hot pasta sitting in front of me. It'd been delicious a moment ago, but now my appetite had disappeared.

My father looked down at his salad and stabbed the bed of lettuce with his fork. "Remove them from the business the way they removed me. Pull the rug out from underneath them. Make them fall on their asses." He took a bite and chewed as he stared at me, his gaze hard with anger.

Relief swept through me, because for just a moment, I'd feared my father had suggested something far more sinister. "I do the books every day, and with the increased revenue, we're making the same that we were making before. The only thing that's really changed is it's far less work than it used to be—"

"It's *my* business," he snapped. "I don't care if it's doing better now than it was before. That's beside the point, and of all people, I'd expect you to understand that. It's our legacy, Scarlett."

My father never snapped at me, but lately, he'd been doing it all the time. "A legacy can be more than just money. It can be family. It can be donations. It can be other things. It doesn't have to be an illegal business—"

"I expected more from you." He set his fork aside, clearly done with his half-eaten meal.

I felt like I'd been slapped.

"We agreed we would take this back together."

"Dad, you have an equal third of the business. You haven't taken a pay cut. Why don't we just…let this go? Live in peace. Remember that Axel only took the business because you cut him out—"

"You've been married to him for a couple weeks, and he's already turned you against me?"

I felt like I'd been slapped again. "We don't talk about you, Dad. And he could never turn me against you." Axel had already whispered rumors into my ear, and I'd ignored them all. "I know where my loyalty lies."

"It doesn't seem like it." He pulled the linen off his lap and set it on the table, telling the waiter he was finished.

"The business is still in our family. That's what you wanted—and we have it."

"You think I would have let you marry him if you were going to turn like this?"

"I'm just being logical."

He didn't raise his voice, but he deepened his tone into a threat. "No one fucks me over and gets away with it. Are you with me or not?"

"Dad, that's ridiculous—"

"Are you or are you not?" he demanded.

"Of course—"

"Then we'll get back what's rightfully ours, and they can eat shit."

The place was so much bigger than my old apartment. Every time I stepped off the elevator and moved into the entryway, surrounded by walls covered in dark wallpaper, mirrors on the walls, a chandelier that hung low, and the vase of lilies in the center of the table, I felt like I was in a museum rather than my home.

I took the stairs to the next level, my feet tired in the heels.

When I made it to the second floor, I approached my suite door and went inside, relieved I wouldn't have to speak to Axel tonight. Not sure how I would keep a straight face after the heated conversation I'd had with my father. I stepped into my bedroom and immediately noticed something had changed.

All my stuff was gone.

I opened the closet—and it was empty.

The bathroom counter was vacant of my brushes and makeup.

Everything had been taken away and cleaned—as if I never lived here.

I marched down the hallway to his bedroom and let myself inside. "Where's my stuff?" I spoke before I even saw him. I shut the door and found him in the living room. There was a glass of scotch on the coffee and a cigar between his fingertips. He was in just his gray sweatpants and nothing else. "Axel?"

He smashed the cigar into the black bowl and extinguished it before he rose to his full height, a living skyscraper. He walked toward me, muscular arms hanging by his sides. "You're living here now."

My eyebrows rose up my face. "That's not what we agreed to—"

"I've been patient with you," he said calmly. "Very fucking patient. But no more."

"And you just get to decide this?" I asked incredulously. "That's not how it works—"

"That *is* how it works," he snapped. "Because you told me you would try, and sleeping down the fucking hall is not trying." His eyes were beautiful on most occasions, but they were livid now. "We sleep together. Period."

"If you'd just asked me, I would have considered it—"

"No, you wouldn't. You needed a push—and I pushed you."

"We had a nice night last night, and now it's ruined—"

"I'm not sleeping without you." He raised his voice now, not quite yelling, but the increase in decibel was still terrifying. "I can't go back now. I want you in my arms, every fucking night, until we die. End of story."

I was so angry I could scream, but the words didn't come.

"I know you liked it."

I turned away, unable to look at his face anymore. I approached the window, seeing the rain on the asphalt reflect the city lights.

When he spoke again, his voice was gentle. "Baby."

I remained at the window, looking into the cold night.

His footsteps sounded, growing louder the closer he approached.

My heart started to race.

Then his chest pressed into my back, and his muscular arms wrapped around me, shielding me from the cold that came in through the windowpane. His head dipped to my neck, and his hands gripped my arms, locking me into his embrace. The thin strap of my dress barely covered my shoulder, so he was able to press a kiss directly to the cold skin.

This was the moment I was supposed to buck him off or storm away, but cocooned against his chest was the most comfortable I'd ever been. My skin hummed to life at his proximity, and I melted into a pile of mush at his feet. He still had that effect on me, inexplicably, even after what he did.

His lips moved near my ear. "Try with me."

"I am."

"Try harder." His arms pulled on me, forcing me to relax fully against him, to trust that his body would support mine. His mouth moved to my shoulder and he kissed me again, squeezed me to him so hard I could feel his heartbeat against my back. "How was dinner?"

A shitshow. "Fine."

"What did you order?"

"The Bolognese,"

He kissed my shoulder again, embracing me with warmth and affection so potent it made me slide further under his spell.

"How was your night?"

"I had a steak and watched the game."

"Sounds nice."

"Thought about you the whole time."

"What did you think about?" I didn't know what possessed me to ask such a risky question, but it came tumbling out. Whenever he was this close to me, I couldn't think straight.

"You really want to know?" He kissed my shoulder again, and I could feel the smile on his lips. "I thought about making you my wife—officially." He kissed my shoulder. "Making you come as you call me your husband."

A rush of heat flushed through me instantaneously, making my neck hot, making my fingertips numb.

"That's what I always think about when I'm alone."

All my toiletries were on his bathroom counter. There were two sinks and plenty of room on either side, so I left my things where they were, washed my face, and removed my makeup. I did my regular evening routine, putting on my hydrator and eye cream, wearing my silk pajamas.

I knew a clean face wouldn't turn him off whatsoever. He'd fucked me with and without makeup, with the same intensity, like there was no difference between the two. In the mirror, I could see the large tub behind me, remember the conversations we'd had, the way he'd held me against his chest.

I'd never been so confused in my life.

I wanted to go in there and jump his bones, but I also wanted him clear across the room at the same time.

I lingered in the bathroom, staring at myself in the mirror, procrastinating.

His voice came in through the crack in the door. "Baby, get your ass in here."

A shiver moved down my spine as I closed my eyes.

"Come on."

I turned off the light and left the bathroom, seeing him propped slightly up on his arm. His bedside lamp was still on, and his eyes followed me as I walked around the bed and moved to my side.

I wore silk pajama shorts and a t-shirt, my bra gone because my tits didn't feel like being restricted tonight. I sat on the edge of the bed, my back to him, and turned off the lamp on my nightstand. My phone was there charging on the tray.

He curled his arm around my stomach and tugged me close, like the kraken pulled ships from the surface deep underwater. He pulled me to the center of the bed, turned off his lamp, and then pressed up against me, his chest to my back, his hard dick digging into my thigh through his shorts.

He crossed his arm over my chest and held me close, as close as we could be and still breathe. Then he went still, his face against the back of my head, the two of us sharing a single pillow.

He didn't make a move.

He just lay with me.

"Goodnight, baby."

I was relieved…but also disappointed. "Goodnight."

I was in the study downstairs when Axel appeared in the open doorway. In a long-sleeved shirt and dark jeans, he looked like he was about to leave for the day. He left all the paperwork to me and did more of the physical stuff related to the business. His eyes were glued to mine as he walked around the back of the couch and approached me at the desk. "I'll be gone most of the day."

I didn't ask where he was going or what he was doing.

He paused, as if he expected me to ask. When I didn't, he moved on. "Call me if you need anything."

"Alright."

He didn't turn away, like he had something else to say. "We're having dinner tonight. Be ready at seven."

"Another dinner party?"

"No, just the two of us."

The invitation felt too heavy to be an innocent dinner. I knew there was more to it than that.

"And when we get home, we're going to fuck."

The heat that surged through me felt like a fiery comet. I stared, dumbfounded, offended and turned on at the same time.

He stared at me like he expected opposition, but when it didn't come, he turned around and left the study.

I wore a black dress with pumps, a gold necklace around my throat. The walk-in closet had a mirror, so I put on my outfit there and checked it in the mirror before I stepped out. It was skintight and left little to the imagination—especially where my tits were concerned.

When I walked out, Axel was on the couch in black jeans and a collared button-down shirt, the sleeves pushed to his elbows like it was a hot summer day. He must have spotted me in his peripheral because he turned off the TV then stood up to face me. When his eyes landed on mine, he stilled and looked me over, from top to bottom, with intense slowness, as if he was undressing me without even touching me.

He came closer, walking up to me, coming so close our lips nearly touched.

I knew what he was going to say before he said it.

"I like that dress." He pulled away, wearing that intense expression, and then that old smile came through, a smile I hadn't seen often since we were married. His hand moved to mine, and he gently tugged me with him.

My heart was in my throat, and I was nervous like I'd never been, like I was about to lose my virginity all over again. The walk to the car was spent in silence, and the drive to the restaurant was spent in silence too. I wasn't sure how I would get through dinner when all I could think about was how he planned to fuck me.

I could put an end to it and say no. He would listen and swallow his disappointment like a gentleman. But the desire clenching between my legs forbade me from saying no. Because it'd been a long time since I'd had a good lay, and despite what Axel had done to me, he would deliver. He always did.

After he pulled out the chair for me, he sat across the table and ordered the wine. The waiter handed out the menus then walked away so we could peruse the options.

I stared at the menu but couldn't really focus on it. When I lifted my gaze just above the top of my menu to look at him, he was already staring at me. My eyes ducked down again like I'd been caught.

"What are you thinking, baby?" The smile was in his voice.

"What happened to not calling me that?"

"We're way beyond that now, sweetheart." He scanned the menu then set it aside.

I didn't even have an appetite. This was just foreplay to me. The way his big body took up the entire chair, the way he took control of the evening and ordered everything, the way his eyes looked in that shirt…

The waiter poured the glasses of wine and asked for our entrées.

"Chicken marsala." Then he gave a slight nod toward me. "She'll have the gnocchi." He handed over the menus.

"You didn't ask what I wanted."

"Did you want something else?"

I didn't say anything.

"We both know it doesn't matter anyway." He brought the glass to his lips and took a sip, that arrogant look in his eyes. He was relaxed in the chair, his shoulders broad, the muscles in his arms stretching the sleeves of his shirt. His clothes were all in bigger sizes because the muscles he carried made him a behemoth. A lot of the other guys I dated on the apps were scrawny…and unremarkable.

He took another drink of his wine as he stared at me.

I didn't know what to say. He made me feel like I was naked in that restaurant, all the goodies out for everyone to see. "What should we talk about?"

"How I'm going to fuck you." He said it with a straight face, pulling off a level of confidence no one else could replicate. "I'd love to talk about that." He swirled his wine as he looked at me, the stare suffocating.

"What if I say no—"

"You won't."

"How do you know—"

"Because I do." The smile returned, arrogant and victorious. "It's our one-month anniversary. You must be going as crazy as I am."

"My hand works just fine, thank you."

"Baby, come on." His grin widened. "We both know it's not even close."

I took a drink of my wine. A big one.

"This is what I'm thinking…"

I wasn't sure if I could listen to this.

"Your dress hiked up with my face between your legs. Start off nice and slow."

Oh Jesus…

"Take my time. Really enjoy it. Because I've missed that pussy."

My legs were already crossed, but I involuntarily squeezed my thighs together.

"Then when you're right there…I'll stop. And you'll beg me to fuck you."

The waiter came over with a basket of bread and placed it in the middle of the table, having no idea what he just stepped into.

Axel stared at me the entire time, as if there had been no interruption.

When the waiter walked away, Axel continued. "Then I'll move between those soft thighs and sink as far as you can handle. You'll wince at my size, you always do, but I'll keep going. After a couple thrusts, I'll come, because fuck, it's been a long time. But I'll still be hard for you, and I'll fuck you until you cry."

I couldn't clench my thighs any more. They were locked tight.

"Unless you have something else in mind, Pretty?"

I'd never been this hot. It felt like a summer afternoon with one hundred percent humidity. It was so suffocating, I could barely breathe. I actually felt the sweat on the back of my neck and knew my hair had started to absorb it. Whenever my fingers traveled underneath my panties, that was the fantasy that came into my mind. Even after a date dropped me off, my thoughts turned to Axel, the man I wished were still mine. The only difference was, in my fantasies, he made me come with his mouth before he shoved that big dick inside me.

He continued to stare at me, as if he expected me to say something to that.

"I do."

He'd been spinning the stem of his glass, but he stopped when he heard what I said.

"If you get to come quick, then so do I…"

He stared at me, all the veins in his neck popping.

"And I want to come against your mouth."

He spoke under his breath so quietly I hardly heard what he said. "Fuck this." He raised his hand and made a gesture to the waiter. "Get me the check."

The second our feet hit the top of the stairs, he lifted me from the floor and had me straddle his hips, his big hands cupping my ass cheeks as they poked out of my rising dress. He kissed me as he squeezed me and carried me at the same time, giving me his tongue right away.

He carried me into the bedroom and kicked the door shut behind us. He could do it all at once, grope my ass, stick his tongue down my throat, and bring me to the bedroom where he would fuck me like he promised.

He gently laid me on the bed before he yanked my dress up, showing my black thong and my belly button. His big hand grabbed the fabric of my panties and tugged them off, nearly ripping them because he didn't wait for me to lift my hips. Then he yanked his shirt open, ripping off all the buttons of his expensive shirt just so he could get naked quicker. It dropped to the floor behind him, his carved body ready to make me come. He loosened his belt and dropped his jeans, taking his boxers along the way.

Oh damn. How could I forget?

That was one hell of a dick.

He was on top of me again, his naked body on mine, his lips searing my mouth once they made contact. When his dick pressed against me, it was hot and throbbing, oozing from the tip like he could barely keep his load in the holster without even being inside me.

Then he moved down, scooped up my hips in his muscular arms, and kissed me.

Kissed me right there.

My head immediately rolled back, and I gripped the bedding on either side of me. "Fuck…" I'd forgotten how this felt. I'd forgotten all the wonderful things he could do with that perfect mouth. A man hadn't offered to go down on me since him, and now that I knew how sexy a man's enthusiasm could be, I never wanted to ask again. I wanted to *be* asked.

He sucked hard with that big mouth, pulling my clit firmly between his lips before he swirled his tongue around my nub, packing his kisses with pressure he wasn't afraid to exert. His thick arms continued to cradle my legs and hold them in position so I could just lie there and enjoy it.

I'd forgotten how good this was.

I had been wet long before we'd gotten to the restaurant, but I'd been soaked after I heard him describe how this night would go, so it really didn't take much for me to feel that exquisite burn between my legs, the fire that would scorch me from head to toe. I was ready for it the moment his hungry mouth met my lips.

It swept through me like a surge through a broken dam, gallons of water breaking free and rushing over me. Tears had formed in my eyes before he had even begun. It was an avalanche of pleasure, starting off slow then snowballing into a boulder of pleasure. "Yes…" I ground my hips against his face, swept away by the most pleasure I'd felt in seven months. It was so raw and intense, so amazing, that I knew why I couldn't get over Axel, because no man had ever made me feel like *this*. "Yes…"

He gave me a final kiss before he moved up my body, his big dick throbbing in desperation. One arm hooked behind my knee, and he opened me so he could shove his big head through my little slit. He kept up the pressure and continued to push, slowly breaking through my entrance and sinking as far as my body would allow.

It hurt exactly as he'd said it would—but I fucking loved it.

With me folded underneath him, he barely made it through a couple pumps before he came, releasing inside me with a sexy moan. He twitched inside me as he released all his desire, his breaths uneven and low like a growl. "Fuck…this pussy." The second it passed, he started to thrust again, just as hard as he'd been when he'd first sunk inside me.

My hand gripped his ass as I tugged him closer to me, wanting him to hurt me with every thrust. My nails dug into his back for purchase, rocking with him to meet his hard thrusts, taking his dick with moans of pain and pleasure.

We moved and moaned like we hadn't already released, like we still had that itch we couldn't scratch. His body quickly became coated in sweat from fucking me so hard, and my pussy quickly turned sore because his dick was like a wrecking ball. But I didn't want it to stop. Now that I had it, I never wanted it to stop.

18

AXEL

She was mine.

Finally.

I lay beside her in bed, the clock on the nightstand showing the late hour. After I fucked her senseless, I fucked her again…and again. The last time I had her was from behind, that beautiful ass right in front of me, my fingers kneading her fine cheeks.

I turned my head to look at her. She was knocked out, her tangled hair across the pillow. Her breaths were deep and even, like she was exhausted.

I wanted to wake her up so I could fuck her again, but I decided to let her sleep.

I fell asleep at some point, and I woke up to the shift of the mattress as she left the bed. My eyes opened to the morning sunshine peeking through the drapes. Her silhouette became visible to me, sitting at the edge of the bed, her long hair trailing down her back.

She stood up to leave.

"Where you going, baby?" I spoke with a raspy voice, barely able to get the words out because my throat was dry. I turned on my side and reached my arm across, my fingers wrapping around her wrist.

She looked at me over her shoulder, her hair a mess, but somehow, she'd never looked more beautiful. "Going to shower."

I tugged her toward me, gently coaxing her back to bed. "You can shower later."

"I have work—"

"You're fired." I pulled her to me, bringing her partially on top of me. When she was near, my hands gripped her sexy curves and brought her closer, my mouth catching a hard nipple. I tasted it, sucked it, gripping her narrow waist as I squeezed her.

"I forgot how frisky you are in the morning."

"Let me remind you." I rolled her onto her back then separated her thighs with my knees, opening her slender body to take me. I licked my hand then wetted the head of my dick before I pushed inside her, seeing her wince because of the soreness. But she didn't ask me to stop, so I continued to sink, burying myself inside her until there was nowhere left to go. I didn't push as hard as I normally would, knowing how sensitive she was after all the fucking last night. I took it slow and easy, being as gentle as I could.

Her winces turned to moans, and her palms planted on my chest as I started to rock, started to thrust into her tightness, immersed in her wetness and my leftover seed from the night before. Then her hips started to move with mine, and our bodies fell into a beautiful synchronicity.

Sex had conquered her barriers, and now I finally saw the woman I used to know, the woman who was open and playful, who let me inside her fully. I'd wanted to fuck her the moment I saw her again, and not just because she was a sexy woman, but because it would finally reconnect us.

And we were definitely connected.

I folded her underneath me and thrust gently, making the headboard tap lightly against the wall. My dick wanted to explode at the sight of her, seeing the heat of arousal in her eyes, the way her cheeks reddened from the rush of blood.

I knew her tells, knew when she was about to come, and I saw the shininess in her eyes from impending tears. Her pussy had tightened too, gripping my dick like a hard handshake. Knowing how close she was made it harder for me to remain steady, to keep the bullet in the barrel, to open the door and let her go first.

Then she came with whimpers and moans, her hips bucking automatically, her tears like diamonds that streaked down her cheeks. Her nails curved and started to dig into my flesh, started to carve her mark into me.

I couldn't keep it together despite all the loads I'd dropped last night. It was like all those fucks never happened. I was careful not to push as hard as I could when I released, remaining delicate with her sore body. She already knew how big my dick was. I didn't have to remind her anymore. "Fuck yeah, baby." I filled my wife with everything I had, like there weren't already loads there. My mouth dropped to hers, and I gave her gentle kisses, feeling her soft lips with mine.

She kissed me back automatically, her claws withdrawing into their sheaths.

I got off her and lay by her side.

She pulled the sheets to her chest and lay there, her eyes heavy like she could drift off to sleep.

"Let's go out to breakfast."

She turned her head to look at me. "What about work?"

"I fired you, remember?"

She smirked in amusement.

"Come on, baby."

"You have a first-class butler to bring you food."

"But if we stay in this room, I'm going to fuck you on every piece of furniture, and I know that pretty pussy needs a break." I leaned over her and pressed a kiss to her shoulder then the top of her chest. "We skipped dinner, so I know you're hungry."

Right on cue, her stomach released a tiny roar.

She chuckled. "Thanks for calling me out, girl."

"Come on." I got out of bed and watched her watch me with the same hunger I wore whenever I looked at her. "Let's go."

I took her to a little café that was mostly deserted because most people didn't go out to brunch on a Thursday. Neither one of us had showered, just brushed our teeth and washed our faces, so she was completely natural, and the way the morning light struck her face was mesmerizing.

She ordered breakfast crepes with a side of bacon and toast.

I ordered a breakfast burger with a side of pancakes.

We both sipped our coffee and took bites of our food, neither one of us saying much.

It felt the way it used to, and I'd thought that would never happen. My alleged betrayal had pushed her too far, and I'd feared I would never be able to pull her back to me. But there she was, sipping her coffee and remaining quiet because it wasn't a tense silence that required forced conversation.

"How's your food?" I asked.

"Why do you think I haven't spoken in ten minutes?"

I smirked.

"I've never heard of this place. It's good."

"I come here once in a while."

"With the other girls who spend the night?" she asked, her voice slightly playful but with a hint of jealous accusation.

"The only women I've taken to breakfast are my first wife and my second wife."

Her eyes lifted from her food and looked at me. "Sometimes I forget you were already married."

"I forget it all the time—thankfully." Scarlett had only married me for the business, but it felt more like a real marriage than it had with my ex-wife. Scarlett refused to drive my expensive cars because she preferred her beat-up car, and she never asked for money or even mentioned our financial situation. I knew she didn't want me for my money. Maybe my dick—but I was okay with that.

We returned to eating in comfortable silence. We were one of the only couples in there, so it felt like we had the café to ourselves. My eyes focused on her face the entire time, unable to believe this moment was real.

She seemed to avoid my gaze, like my stare was too much. "What are your plans for the day?"

"Work."

"What exactly do you do when you're gone all day?"

"Sometimes I'm meeting with distributors. Sometimes I'm with Theo. And sometimes I'm managing my other interests."

"What other interests do you have?"

"The trust that has been in my family for generations. The olive oil, the hotels, shit like that…"

"Oh, that's right. Do you interact with your parents when you do that?"

"Not really. I take care of my stuff, and they take care of theirs," I said. "One of our assets is an old gallery that's been in Florence for hundreds of years. It's available for private events but open to the public on occasion. I also have assets in France, so sometimes I'll travel up there for a couple of days."

"That sounds like a lot. I'm surprised you even got involved with my father."

"I know my parents have been trying to find every loophole they possibly can to get rid of me, so I've decided to diversify myself a bit."

Her eyes dropped in pity. "I'm sorry."

It made me feel like shit, but knowing she cared made it a lot more tolerable. "It doesn't bother me."

"Yes, it does," she said quietly. "And it's okay if it bothers you." Her eyes lifted to look at mine, beautiful on this winter morning. "I know I would be devastated if that happened with my father."

I was tempted to tell her the truth, to tell her what her father had done and ask her to keep it a secret, but as much as I trusted her, I wasn't sure if I could trust her with that. She would never confront her father if she knew mine would be killed, but she would tip her hand in other ways. Dante was smart, and he would immediately notice if his daughter started to pull away from him, looked at him differently, spoke to him differently. "We've never discussed the financial aspect of this marriage." We hadn't really been talking before the wedding. Well, she hadn't really been talking to me, at least.

"Let's keep it separate." She blew on her coffee before she took a drink because it was still hot, even on this cold morning. "I assumed that's what we would do."

"Why would you assume that?"

She took another drink before she returned the mug to the table. "I have my stuff, and you have yours."

"That's not how marriage works." And she didn't have much. Dante had hoarded all the wealth and made her jump through hoops for pennies. "And that's definitely not how I want this marriage to work."

"Well, I think I should receive a salary for handling all the paperwork for the business. And I'd like it to be competitive, a lot more than what my father was paying me."

"We'll split my share."

She was about to reach for her coffee again but hesitated. "Since these are your connections and you're the one doing the more dangerous work, I don't think that's fair. What about twenty-five percent?"

"Fifty-fifty."

"I don't think that's fair—"

"And I don't think it's fair that your father was paying you cents on the euro."

Her stare hardened for a few seconds. "Even if that's true, it's not your obligation to make up for that—"

"I'm your husband. Anything that concerns you is my obligation."

"Axel, I want to work for my money, not receive a handout—"

"It comes out to fifty-fifty anyway since we're married. There's no way around it, baby."

"We keep our financials separate. I get my paycheck. There's no reason anything needs to be fifty-fifty."

"Why are you resisting this?"

She stilled at the abrupt question.

"We're married. My money is your money. I want you to have it."

"And I want my own money, Axel. You already let me live there rent-free—"

"Let you live there…" I released a chuckle because that was ridiculous. "Baby, it's your home."

"You know what I mean. And after what happened in your previous marriage, I would assume you'd prefer to keep everything separate."

"I don't compare you to her. I'm not going into my second marriage thinking about the bullshit from my first. It's different with you, and I have no doubt that you want me for me and not my wallet."

Her eyes immediately dropped to stare into the contents of her mug, like my words provoked her in some way. "We both know I only married you to reclaim the business."

"That was the excuse that got you in the door. But that's not the reason you're sitting across from me now. It's not the reason you slept with me last night. Everything is different now."

Her eyes remained down.

"You continue to drive that piece-of-shit car when I've offered any of mine—"

"There's nothing wrong with my car."

"You're the wife of a billionaire—start acting like it."

"I like my car."

"Well, I don't."

"You're being a snob."

"I want my wife to accept the gifts I offer. That doesn't make me a snob. I've worked hard for the things I have, and I want to share them with you."

Her eyes remained down.

"Look at me."

There was a beat before she obeyed, before she lifted her gaze and focused on mine.

"Stop resisting."

Her eyes glanced away momentarily before she spoke. "I appreciate your generosity, but I prefer to keep things separate. I want to earn my own money. I've never really had the opportunity before."

Because her father was an asshole. "And what will you do with it?"

"I don't ask you what you do with your money."

"I'm just curious."

Her eyes shifted back and forth between mine. "Invest in property…grow my wealth."

"Why do you need to grow your wealth when you're married to a billionaire?"

"Because it's not my money—"

"It *is* your money." I didn't want to ruin our breakfast, the morning after a passionate night, but her words were like a slap across the face. "Unless…" I turned quiet, the truth dawning on me as I held her stare. "You think this marriage is temporary…"

She broke eye contact instantly. "I just—"

"I meant what I said. I've pardoned your father once, but I won't pardon him again. If he crosses me, his head is gone. Do you understand me?" I spoke at a regular volume in the café, not caring if anyone overheard me.

Of course, she looked horrified. "Axel—"

"Do you understand me?"

"Let's stop with the threats—"

"Don't cross me, Scarlett." I rose to my feet and nearly tipped the chair over with the force. I left her there, surrounded by the dirty plates from the breakfast feast we'd just enjoyed, and stormed off.

I stayed out of the house for the day and most of the night.

She called me twice, several hours apart, and I ignored those calls. There were no texts.

When I came home, it was almost midnight. I walked past the guest bedroom where she had stayed when she first moved in, and I wondered if she'd moved her stuff back while I was gone.

I walked into my bedroom, expecting it to be quiet and dark, but the lamps were on, and the TV illuminated the walls with the flashing light. My eyes turned to the couch, seeing her there with a blanket over her body.

I stared for several seconds, surprised to see her awake long after her usual bedtime.

She stared back, hesitance in her position.

I walked past her and headed to the bedroom so I could kick off my boots and ditch all the clothes I wore. I hadn't showered since yesterday, so I shut the bathroom door and stood under the warm water longer than I normally would. The sight of her should make me burn in excitement, but my anger was too potent.

I left the towel on the floor for Aldo to grab tomorrow and headed back into the bedroom.

She sat on the edge of the bed, wearing her silk pajamas, her long legs crossed.

Buck naked, I turned my back to her and pulled out a pair of boxers from the dresser. The drawer slid open and shut, and the TV was no longer audible in the next room because she'd switched it off. I pulled them on then turned to her.

Her gaze faltered under my heavy stare, the intensity too much for her to absorb.

"If you have something to say, say it," I snapped. "I'm fucking tired." I wasn't tired at all, and I wasn't sure how I would sleep next to her tonight. Not because I wanted her, but because, for the first time, I *didn't* want her.

She got to her feet and came close, a foot shorter than me without her usual heels. "Just because we slept together doesn't mean everything is fixed between us. It doesn't mean I trust you. It doesn't mean I've forgiven you. You expect me to embrace all the elements of marriage, when I'm still taking it a day at a time."

I was still irrationally angry, even if her explanation was sound.

"Don't rush me. It's not going to make this go any faster."

My eyes shifted away as I released a heavy sigh. I just wanted the woman in front of me, all of her, and I wanted her to want all of me too. I wanted her to let me take care of her. I wanted her to trust me as blindly as she did before.

"I want my own money—and I want to earn it. I won't apologize for that."

I gave a slight nod in acknowledgment. "And I just want to share mine with you."

Her eyes softened. "Maybe we'll get there someday… but not today."

I released a heavy breath of disappointment. "Goodnight, then."

"Axel, why are you still mad at me?"

"I'm not mad at you."

"You clearly are—"

"I'm mad at the situation."

"The situation that you caused."

I clenched my teeth and sucked in a breath that sounded like a hiss. It took all my strength not to say anything, to keep my mouth shut, to let her believe that fucking nonsense. I looked away and avoided her stare, unsure if I could restrain the truth this time. I continued to protect my parents, when Scarlett was the person I needed most. It was so fucked up.

She continued to stare at the side of my face. "What is it?"

I stepped away. "Nothing."

"It's not nothing." Her eyes followed me.

"I'm going to sleep." I sat on my side of the bed and turned off the lamp. My phone had a ton of texts and emails, but I wasn't in the mood to look at that right now. I kicked back the covers and got under the sheets, immediately closing my eyes in the hope Scarlett would leave me alone.

A moment later, the other lamp turned off, and her lithe body dipped the mattress.

I didn't smother her with affection. I didn't try to fuck her. An invisible line was drawn in the center, and I wouldn't cross it. I hoped she didn't either.

Minutes passed, and I couldn't fall asleep, not when I was this bitter and angry.

Then the mattress shifted as her weight moved… closer to me. Her arm slid over my torso, and her cheek rested on my shoulder. She snuggled into me, tucking her leg between my knees.

I wanted to push her off, but I couldn't.

I couldn't because I fucking wanted it.

She turned her cheek and pressed a warm kiss to my shoulder then another to the top of my chest.

My body burned several degrees hotter, and my boxers got snug. It might seem like just a couple of kisses, but they were the same kisses she used to give me in the dark, quiet invitations.

"I'm sorry that I upset you." Her voice was a whisper, her breath falling across my skin.

I turned my head and grazed her hairline with my mouth. "Prove it."

She stilled at my words, her lips against my shoulder.

I could feel her heart race quicker, feel the sudden spike in its beats. She was warmer too, as if her body had just put out a blast of heat.

Then she lifted herself onto her elbow so her face hovered above mine. Her hair fell down around me like a curtain. Her soft fingertips cupped the side of my face, and she kissed me, bringing those lips as soft as angel wings against my mouth. It was hesitant at first, like she couldn't truly embrace the moment without feeling the guilt, but that hesitation faded fast, and then her kiss deepened. Her mouth parted farther, and she reciprocated my passion, her tongue meeting mine before our lips came apart and then reunited.

I rolled her onto her back and tugged down her cute little shorts until there was nothing underneath me but her flesh.

She pushed down my shorts and let me kick them to the bottom of the bed.

I positioned her underneath me, the sheets to my waist, and with my eyes on hers, I sank. Inch by inch, I entered her tightness and was coated in her wetness. Her breaths became uneven and raspy, her body clearly still sore from the night before. I made it in, careful not to push too hard and hurt her.

She released a deep breath when I was fully inside her, her arms hooked behind my shoulders, her knees squeezing my torso. With desire burning in her eyes like fire and her lips parted in anticipation of another kiss, she looked at me in that special way that made me feel alive.

My thrusts started, slow and easy, and my lips dipped to hers so I could kiss her. The kiss was more important than the union of our bodies below the waist. I focused on that, feeling her lips and the way they trembled, appreciating the little moans she made.

Her nails continued to slice into my back, digging so deep that the sweat poured in and burned. The anger from our conversation was long gone now that I was deep in the throes of passion with the only woman I wanted. Strangers had stayed in my bed in her absence, but they were all a means to an end. With Scarlett, I wanted to slow it down instead of rush to the finish line. I wanted to kiss her instead of choke her. I wanted to make her want me the way I wanted her.

SCARLETT

The guilt.

It was starting to eat me alive.

My father considered himself an intelligent man, but Axel was brilliant. His easygoing attitude and charming smile made him seem harmless, but underneath that warmth was a man who always stayed ahead of the game.

I meant what I'd said, that I needed more time to settle into our marriage before we consolidated additional aspects of our lives, but another part of me knew I also refrained because it was a temporary arrangement. That I'd only said yes, knowing there would be a way out sometime in the future.

Now I felt like shit about it.

I shouldn't feel bad at all, not when he'd leveraged my family legacy against me to force me into marriage, a marriage I would have willingly committed to if he hadn't broken my heart. But I did feel bad about it. Really bad.

Because I cared about him so much, as much as I'd always had.

Axel was gone, so I stopped by my father's place. Guards still dotted the property, so that aspect hadn't changed. I let myself inside, said hello to his assistant, and then saw my father in the study a moment later.

"Hello, sweetheart." Our last conversation had been strained and contentious, but his affectionate warmth had returned as if it had never happened. "What a nice surprise." He sat behind his desk and clicked his mouse a couple times, closing out of the windows on his screen before he gave me his full attention.

"I finished work early today. Thought we could get lunch."

"That means Axel's not home?"

"He's usually gone most of the day. He leaves pretty early."

"And where does he go?"

"He doesn't tell me, and I don't ask." I had a feeling those types of questions would be unwelcome, especially after the fight we'd had.

My father ended that line of questioning. "Where do you want to go?"

"I always pick, Dad."

"And that's how it should be." He rose from his chair. "So, where are we headed?"

"Pino's? I'm in the mood for a sandwich."

"A sandwich, it is."

One of his drivers took us into town and dropped us off so we could walk the rest of the way, moving down the cobblestone street as others passed on foot or bicycle. We reached the little sandwich shop, a hole-in-the-wall but a famous spot, and we each got a huge sandwich we would never finish. We sat at a small table outside, pigeons dropping down whenever a crumb got loose.

My father took a big bite then wiped his mouth with a napkin.

"No salad today?" I teased.

He smirked then finished chewing. "Wasn't an option."

"Dad, you're in great shape. You can get a sandwich once in a while."

"Thank you, sweetheart," he said. "But once you're my age, you'll realize how few sandwiches you can eat."

"Forty is the new thirty."

"But it's not the new twenty."

We ate in silence for a while, enjoying the fat sandwiches that no one could eat on their own. Well, except Axel. That man ate more than anyone I knew, but he still had no body fat because of all those muscles. All those sexy muscles that drove me wild.

I tried not to think about it, especially when I was with my father. "How are things going with production?"

He finished his bite before he returned the half-eaten sandwich to the paper wrapping and wiped his fingers clean of the mustard stains. "As happy as I am that the business has expanded at such a quick rate, fulfilling the product demand is another story. My facility can only produce so much at the moment. It's not easy hiring the right people. Not like I can post the job online or something. And getting the Colombians to sell me more product has its challenges."

"What challenges?" I asked. "Their biggest account just got bigger."

"They ask a lot of questions."

"What kinds of questions?"

"They want to know why we suddenly need double the quantity overnight."

"It's none of their business."

"I agree," he said. "But that doesn't mean they aren't curious."

"So, did they agree?"

"Yes, but they increased their rate."

Once they knew business was even better, they wanted a bigger piece of the pie. It was a reasonable request, but it was annoying, nonetheless. For us to make the same amount, we'd have to increase the price to customers, which we'd already recently done. We couldn't add another price increase so soon, so we'd have to eat the cost. "How much?"

"Ten percent."

"*What?*"

"I know."

"And you agreed?"

He nodded.

"Five percent is more reasonable."

"Well, they weren't in the mood to negotiate."

"Do Axel and Theo know this?"

"Not yet."

Axel would be pissed. "They won't take that well."

"They know it comes with the territory."

I picked up my sandwich again to take one more bite, even though I was full. Their sandwiches were just so good. "When are you going to tell them?"

He shrugged. "Whenever I see them next. What do you see in the books?"

"Money is good, really good."

"At least there's that."

"Axel offered to split his earnings with me." I wasn't sure what prompted me to blurt that out. Wasn't sure if my father would be pleased or annoyed by that information.

I didn't get an answer—because all he did was stare.

"I told him twenty-five percent was more reasonable."

"It's *your* business." He wasn't warm anymore, cold like the gray clouds above our heads. "You should take it all."

"I thought fifty percent was pretty generous."

"The business means nothing to him. It's just a way to get back at me."

I shouldn't have said anything.

"He's involved in other things. The business isn't his priority, just another hustle. And he wants me to know that."

"I think he just wants to share it with me." I couldn't stop myself from saying the words, from saying something that would definitely offend my father.

My father's stare was far colder than the winter air. "He's manipulating you, sweetheart."

"Manipulating me, how?"

"To turn against me," he said. "That's the final part of his plan, to take you away. It seems to be working."

"Dad, I already said we don't talk about you," I said. "I know you don't like him, but I don't think he's as bad as you think he is. When he offered me half his share, I don't think he had an ulterior motive."

He looked away, his hard jaw clenched. "You're quick to forget he served two years in prison for rape and assault. But no, he's not capable of manipulation?"

"I think he's innocent."

He inhaled a deep breath like he wanted to scream, but he let the pressure hurt his lungs instead. "You're too smart for this, sweetheart. You sat across from me at the table and told me about your relationship with Axel, and he walked in the door with another woman. But you think he's innocent?" His eyes flicked back to me.

A fist punched me right in the heart. "Those two incidents aren't comparable—"

"They still show his character. They show he's a liar and a cheater."

It took all my strength to keep a straight face, to block out the hurt that wanted to bury itself in my heart.

"He's manipulating you, sweetheart."

I trusted my father above everyone else. He was an extraordinary judge of character. He always put me first, even at the expense of his own happiness. But despite all of that, I couldn't agree.

Because I still believed Axel was more than that.

Axel would see right through my façade, so I wanted to avoid him—but there was no avoiding that man. There was nowhere I could run where he wouldn't find me. There was no smile I could fake to deceive him.

I was on the couch when he walked inside, in nothing but workout shorts, the skin over his bulging muscles tinted red from all the blood pumping. His body glistened with sweat, and his hair was slick against his head because it was soaked. He finished off his protein shake when he walked inside and left the empty container on the table.

I was quiet, just staring at him, six foot four of muscle and masculinity.

His arms hung by his sides as he looked at me, covered in rivers of plump veins. "How was your day?"

The sight of him was practically pornographic. His arms alone...

He continued to stare at me. "Baby?"

"Hmm?"

"I asked how your day was."

"Oh…fine." I didn't ask how his was. My throat was so dry, it was like sandpaper.

That arrogant but charming smirk moved over his handsome face. "I'm going to hit the shower. You're welcome to join me." He left my sight and entered the bedroom.

It only took me a couple seconds to follow him, but instead of joining him in the shower, I turned on the faucet in the tub to fill it. After I squirted some bubble bath, the liquid mixed with the water, and the smell of rose hips filled the air.

Axel's back was to me, and he dipped his head to let the water soak his hair. His back was muscular and tight, all the lines that separated the muscles on either side of his spine distinct and pronounced.

I stripped out of my clothes and slipped inside the tub, even though it was only a quarter of the way full. My tits were exposed to the air, and the tops of my legs were covered in bumps. But it had a great view, so I didn't mind sitting there waiting for the water to rise.

He grabbed the bar of soap and scrubbed his body everywhere, rubbing it against his chest and stomach before moving to his arms. Then he cleaned his dick and balls, based on the way he held himself. He did his legs next then lathered shampoo into his hair. When he was ready to rinse, he turned around, exposing his front, more lines of segregated muscles visible. His eyes found mine through the foggy glass, and then the corner of his mouth lifted in a smirk.

The water had risen farther, covering my stomach and legs, except for my bent knees. My chest was still exposed. I had a front-row seat to the sexiest show, and I didn't even have to pay for it.

He dipped his head back and closed his eyes, letting the soap disappear down his back. His hands swiped at his face, pushing aside the extra water that got into his eyes. Then he grabbed the handle and shut off the water, the backdrop of falling water gone, only the echoes left behind.

He stepped out, scrubbed his hair dry with the towel, and then headed for the tub.

"What are you doing?"

"You didn't join me, but I'll join you." He dropped into the opposite end of the tub, making the water rise so high that I had to turn off the faucet. He propped a towel behind his head, his shoulders above the water, and relaxed, his arms on the sides of the tub.

I felt like I was back in time. The only thing that had changed was the length of his hair—and the black wedding ring on his left hand.

Ever since I'd moved in to his suite, I hadn't removed mine. It felt so alien and heavy, but now, it had become a part of me. If it were ever missing, I would know, because my hand would feel five times lighter.

He studied me across the tub, his stare hard like always. "Should we order a pizza?"

"I mean…I'm not going to say no to pizza."

He smirked before he reached for his phone and sent a message to his live-in butler, the nice man whose entire purpose centered around Axel's happiness. If Axel asked him to go find the perfect hooker, Aldo would probably comb the streets for the woman and escort her right to Axel's bed.

When Axel was finished, he looked at me again, his eyes drinking me in.

My hair was pulled up in a tight bun on top of my head to keep it dry. Earrings were still in my lobes. It'd been a cold day on the streets of Florence, and the warm water helped me thaw. But what made me melt was that heated stare.

"You like what you saw?"

"Even if I were gay, I would have liked what I saw."

That cocky smirk was there—as usual.

"I know I should work out."

"For your health, yes. But for your appearance, I wouldn't worry about it."

"I have an ass and a stomach."

His grin widened. "You think I mind?"

My husband had a perfect body, worked out every day, and ate clean most of the time, possessing incredible discipline…and I ate an entire pizza myself most days. The fact that he was as attracted to me as I was to him was a mystery to me. "I've always wanted to get in shape, but then I see the couch…and think about pizza, and all those ambitions go out the window."

"You don't need those ambitions, baby. You're perfect."

The water suddenly felt several degrees warmer. It pressed against me like a heated blanket. "You're the one who's perfect, and I know that takes hard work."

"Once it's a habit, it's not work anymore." His cocky grin should be present, but now he looked serious, staring at me so hard, it seemed as if his mind was not in the conversation. He was thinking about me, not his workout routine. "Watch me tomorrow. I'll flip that tire for you."

The heat that rose up my neck practically burned my skin. I had nowhere to turn, nowhere to hide my face, not when I was stuck across the tub from him. All I could do was clear my throat slightly and look away.

He stared at me, his arms on the sides of the tub like he sat on a throne. "What'd you do for lunch today?"

My eyes moved back to his.

"Aldo said you went out."

"You ask him to keep tabs on me?"

He smirked. "Calm down, baby. He mentioned it in passing."

"I went out to lunch with my father."

He had no reaction to that. "And where did you guys go?"

"Pino's."

"They have damn good sandwiches." His hand moved to his chin, scratching the tip like an itch bothered him.

"And they're huge, hence the stomach and ass."

He grinned. "And tits. Can't forget those." His eyes glanced down at the water, where my chest was hidden beneath the bubbles on the surface.

I smirked as I rolled my eyes.

"I need to fuck those tits sometime."

"I don't know if they're big enough for that." His dick was huge, and my chest was average size.

"They're plenty big, baby." His phone lit up, so he grabbed it and typed a quick message with a single hand. "Aldo is about to walk in. Make sure my girls are covered up."

I moved the bubbles around, hiding all my goodies from the surface.

He didn't bother to hide his junk.

Aldo walked in with the meal, a bottle of wine with two glasses, a bottle of scotch and a short glass, and then a stand that elevated the pizza from the tile floor. He set it all up, careful not to look at either of us, and then walked out.

"That's a nice perk about being married to you," I said. "Getting hot pizza delivered straight to the tub."

"It's not all the good sex?" He grabbed a slice and took a bite, his elbow propped on the side.

I grabbed my own slice then took a bite. "That's second to this."

He chuckled before he took another bite. "Food over sex, huh?"

"Yep. My stomach will agree."

We ate our pizza, and Axel poured the wine. We fell into comfortable silence, both of us eating the fresh pizza that his chef had whipped up from scratch. It was a relaxing end to a long day. This was exactly what I needed after the tension with my father.

"How are things with your father?"

I stared at the slice in my hand, thinking about what he'd said about the Colombians wanting a ten percent increase in revenue. "I always have to walk on eggshells around him. I miss the way it used to be, when I could just be myself without having to worry about provoking him."

"How do you provoke him?"

"You."

He finished his slice and didn't reach for another. "And what did you say about me?"

"Nothing important."

He stared me down across the tub, his eyes applying pressure with their strength.

"I mentioned you offered to split your cut with me down the middle."

"And why would that not be well received?"

"Thinks you're manipulating me."

"Manipulating you to do what?" he asked. "You're already married to me. Already fucking me."

"He thinks you're trying to turn me against him."

A slow smile crept on to his lips.

"What?"

The smile disappeared. "Nothing."

"Doesn't look like nothing."

He looked away, his arms dangling over the sides. "I know you don't want to listen to me insult your father, so let's leave it where it lies." He reached for his wine and took a drink.

"He's just paranoid, always been that way."

"They say when people are paranoid about you crossing them, it's because they've already thought about crossing you."

"What are you saying?"

"That people who are suspicious about their partners cheating are the ones already doing the cheating."

We'd just taken a turn down a seedy street, and I chose to let the silence defeat it.

He took another drink of his wine. "It seemed like you were in a bad mood when I walked inside."

"I didn't say anything."

"But I know you."

"We've only been living together for a week—"

"But I knew you from before. Learned all your tells and all your moods."

"My father and I...we just don't agree on a lot of things when it comes to you."

He set his glass down and stared at me.

"He thinks you're guilty."

"I know he does."

"And I just...don't." I knew how stupid I looked, believing Axel when he gave me no reason to—but I just did. "And that upsets him."

"If he really thought I smacked my wife around, why would he let me marry you?"

My eyes darted elsewhere.

"Now your safety isn't an issue when his company is on the line?" He shook his head. "Or he doesn't believe it, but uses it as an excuse."

"I don't know why that would be the case—"

"So then, it's the first one," he snapped. "He doesn't care if you're marrying a rapist because his company is more important than your safety."

My father was constantly a wedge between us. Always would be. "I told him I believed you, and then he threw the Cassandra incident in my face."

His fingers immediately swiped across his mouth and jawline, his teeth clenched so hard the veins started to pop up his neck. "I'm sure he did."

"I hate this," I said quietly. "That my husband and father can't tolerate each other."

He stared at his glass, his eyes angry. "That's something I can't fix for you."

"I know."

"And even if I could..." His elbow was propped, and his fingertips were against his lips. "I don't think I would."

20

AXEL

I drove through the gates and entered his estate.

Being on his property always gave me a sense of displeasure, but it was overshadowed by the memory of the first time I saw Scarlett. The second I laid eyes on her, I felt all the things a man should feel for his future wife. She hadn't even said a word to me, and I was fucking smitten.

Now she was my wife, waiting at home for me this very instant.

I entered the parlor and took a seat. His butler brought me a drink, which I declined.

Never drink the food or wine of your enemies.

Ten minutes later, he finally entered the parlor, wearing a jacket over his collared shirt and dark jeans. It was nine in the evening, so he should be in sweatpants and a t-shirt, but he chose to dress up, like his clothes would impress me.

I was in sweatpants and a long-sleeved shirt because I didn't give a fuck.

He sat across from me and glanced at the table, seeing that I hadn't accepted a drink. "I'm not going to poison you, Axel."

"I'm sure, Dante."

A heavy moment of silence passed between us. Hostile stares ensued.

Dante was the first to speak. "Will Theo be joining us?"

"He's got other shit to do."

He gave a slight nod.

"What did the Colombians say?"

He crossed his leg, resting one ankle on the opposite knee, a pompous prick. "Once I asked for more product, they asked more questions, and now they're asking for a ten-percent increase."

I laughed at the absurdity.

"The only way I'd ask for more product is if I'm selling more product. So they know business is good."

"Doesn't matter if our business is good. They get paid for their contribution. End of story."

"They say they're more than a supplier, but a valuable member of the team."

I released another laugh. "They've got some gall."

"I told them we would consider it."

"The answer is no."

"We can't say no," Dante said. "That won't go over well. I say we counter at five percent."

"They make the product, and they get paid. They aren't getting a cut of our business."

"Then let's offer to pay more for their product—"

"Why are you being a little bitch?"

Dante's jaw noticeably hardened.

"You've run this business on your own for twenty years?" I asked incredulously. "By being a little bitch?

What about your facility? Increase production at your warehouse."

"I can't do that in this short amount of time," he snapped. "I don't have the manpower or the resources."

I gave an angry sigh. "They get two and a half percent in addition to their base pay. That's it."

"That's a lot less than what they're asking for—"

"If they're going to be that difficult, we'll go to another producer."

"I wouldn't be surprised if the Colombians destroy them to get the business back. You don't know these guys like I do. They can be a huge pain in the ass when they want to be. We're making so much money that we won't even notice—"

"What happens when they ask for more?" I demanded. "And then more?"

"We would deny them. But for now, I think we have no other choice."

"Listen to me, asshole," I snapped. "I don't bend for people. Why? Because they'll bend you all the way over and fuck you in the ass. Give them a little rope, and they'll yank the whole thing."

"I agree," he said. "But since it's their product we're selling, we're at their mercy. I think it's fair to view them as a partner, considering this entire business is based on something they created. I don't like it. But that is a fact."

I rolled my eyes. "You're fucking weak."

"I'm reasonable, and you're a fucking hothead."

"No, I just have a damn spine," I retorted. "Two and a half percent. That's it."

Dante reached for the cigar beside him and lit up, like he needed the smoke to clear his rage. He didn't offer me one, and after tasting the smoke on his tongue, he released it toward the ceiling.

"You failed."

His eyes drifted back to me, the cigar in his mouth.

"You tried to take her away from me, tried to turn her against me, but you can't. Because she fucking sees me. She sees past the bullshit and the lies. She sees who I really am inside. With every passing day, I'm fixing what you broke, and I know one day we'll have what was denied to us. You can't stop it."

He stared at me, smoke rising to the ceiling.

"You can't fucking stop it."

When I got home, Scarlett was already in bed.

She was on her side, the sheets pulled up to her shoulder, all the lights off.

I dropped my clothes in the middle of the floor and tugged off my boots before I got into bed. My phone was put on do not disturb so it wouldn't vibrate all night and cast an annoying light that brightened the ceiling.

I lay there on my back, staring at the dark ceiling, tired but pulsing with life.

I listened to her breathe on the other side of the bed, slow and gentle, rhythmic.

I crossed the mattress and moved up against her, my arm hooking around her stomach and pulling her into me like a bear with its mate. My face entered her hair, and I smelled the flowers and sunshine.

Her body stretched and shifted against me, stirring at my touch.

My fingers hooked into her panties and pulled them over her ass and down her thighs, exposing that fine piece of ass that I wanted to bite.

She stirred a little more, waking up to my hand underneath her shirt, gripping her tit in my big hand.

"Axel…" My name barely left her lips because her voice was so raspy.

I rolled her onto her stomach, her shirt pushed up so her tits were against the mattress, and then I straddled her ass and shoved my dick in the warmth between her cheeks. She had an ass on her, so it was like the perfect home for my dick.

Her breathing elevated, and now she was fully awake, propping herself on her forearms so her hair tumbled down her back.

I slicked the head of my cock before I aimed for her slit, her closed legs making the entrance tighter than usual. It took several tries to push through, but with every thrust, she released a deep breath in anticipation.

I finally made it in and sank nice and slow, feeling her cheeks against my pelvis, her skin soft and warm. "Fuck, Pretty…" My hands tightened into fists as I held myself on top of her, my head above hers, her pussy tighter than it'd ever been.

I thrust into her hard, forcing her clit against the mattress underneath her, and she instantly gave a gasp when she felt me push inside her so forcefully. Her breathing was different. Her moans were different. She'd never had me at this angle, her thighs tight together, barely big enough to contain all of me.

But I knew she liked it, because she was so fucking wet.

Every thrust was like a bullet out of a gun, hard and quick, my hips making her ass jiggle. The heat rushed through me right away, the pleasure so strong that I wanted to stuff her with the first load of the night already.

But her moans had gotten louder, and her voice had already started to crack. I could tell she was there, just by the tightness of her cunt alone. Her slickness continued to flow, coating my dick and reducing the friction even more. Soon, our wet bodies were making sounds as loud as our moans.

Thankfully, she came, her moans bouncing off the headboard and coming back to me in echoes. I could hear the tears in her broken voice, could see the way her nails clawed at the tight sheet over the mattress.

"You like this, baby?" I dipped my lips to her ear.

She finished, her breaths still haywire. "Yes…"

"Tell me you love it." My dick was so hard now, ready to explode inside her paradise.

"I love it."

Fuck. I gave my final pumps. One. Two. Three. Then I shoved myself as deep as I could go, making her cry out slightly as I gave her my load, filling her completely with my seed. Every second of fucking felt so damn good, but when I came inside her, that was the cherry on the sundae.

I remained inside her and continued to grind, sliding through my own come. "Want me to fuck you again?" My lips were back at her ear, my big dick still inside her tightness.

"Yes."

"Ask me."

She hesitated, suddenly embarrassed.

"Ask me."

"Will—will you fuck me like that again?"

A victorious shiver moved down my spine. "I'd love to, Pretty." I started to thrust again, hitting her as hard as last time. I thrust. "Fucking—" I thrust again, driving hard into the mattress. "Love—" I ground my hips, feeling her cheeks right against me, hearing her gasp every time I thrust. "To."

I sat in the armchair, listening to the wind and rain hit the windows hard. A fire was in the hearth, prepared by Aldo before I even walked into the room. I sat there in jeans and a long-sleeved shirt, my heart blocked and fortified before Lorenzo even stepped into the room.

He entered a moment later, wearing a suit, with his eyeglasses on the bridge of his nose. He skipped the pleasantries and sat across from me, setting his bag on the floor beside him. He pulled out a folder full of papers and flipped through them to find what he needed.

These meetings used to take place with my parents and their lawyers.

Now, it was an obnoxious game of telephone.

Lorenzo handed me a sheet. "These are all the events the properties have booked for the month. The hotels have a low occupancy because of the season, so they're considering a few promotions to drive traffic."

I took the sheet and set it aside.

"Prime Minister Amato is coming to Florence and has requested a private event at the art gallery…" His voice trailed off in hesitation, like whatever else he had to say was about to make my life complicated. "He's requested both of you to be present. Because of the long-standing history between your families."

I smirked. "I bet Dad didn't like that."

"He's drafted up his terms for the event."

"Let me guess. Stay at least fifty feet from him at all times, like a fucking restraining order."

He opened the folder again and placed the court order signed by the judge in front of me. "Because of your criminal history, it was granted."

I smirked again, but I was dead inside. "If only they knew…"

"Knew what?"

That I continued to keep both of them alive at the cost of my own happiness. "Nothing."

Lorenzo continued. "You're to stay at least fifty feet away from them—"

"The venue isn't even fifty feet wide."

He paused as he considered that information then made a note on his paper. "They ask for no contact whatsoever. You do not speak to them, and they do not speak to you."

"Fine."

"If the prime minister invites you both into a conversation, you opt out."

"Sure, whatever."

He continued to read through the list, all the demands pretty much the same but worded differently. "They asked you to sign this." He uncapped his pen and pushed the paper toward me.

I snatched it and scribbled my signature. "There you go."

He left the check on the table, my portion of the earnings through the trust. "Goodbye, Mr. Moreau."

I gave him a thumbs-up. "See you, Lorenzo."

He left the parlor, and Aldo let him out.

I didn't move from my armchair, ignoring the check that would take me weeks to deposit. Truth be told, I didn't even care about the money, but if I allowed them to cut me out, I would have no connection to them at all.

I wasn't sure how long I sat there. My phone vibrated a couple times, but I didn't dig it out of my pocket. Nothing seemed important right now, only sulking in my own misery.

"Aldo, have you seen Axel?" Scarlett's distant voice came from far down the hallway. "He's not texting me back, and he always texts me back."

"I believe he's in the parlor, Mrs. Moreau."

"Oh…thank you." Her footsteps were quiet, but they slowly became more pronounced, the thuds audible against the carpet. Then she rounded the corner and looked into the parlor, facing me head on.

It was just like the night she'd shown up to confront me. The rain hit the windows hard. The fire cast shadows in the corners. She'd been the one in a callous mood, but now I was the one who'd bottled my ferocity.

She slowly crept into the room, her eyes shifting back and forth as she absorbed my foul mood. She stopped next to the other chair, the one my lawyer had just occupied. Silence stretched for seconds as she looked at me. "Everything alright…?"

"I just received a restraining order from my parents."

She didn't say a word, but she somehow conveyed an entire conversation with her face, moving through shock, mild surprise, raw offense, and then lingering sadness. "Do you want to be alone?"

Under normal circumstances, I probably wouldn't have spoken to anyone for days, bottling the moment and letting it poison my organs in silence. But there was something about Scarlett that made me feel differently, that made me want to pull her close rather than push her away. "No."

She sat in the armchair across from me, her eyes dropping down to the copy of the court order. She stared at it for several seconds before she lifted her eyes and looked at me again. "All I ever say is sorry… but I don't know what else to say."

"Fuck them. You could say that."

She smiled slightly.

I smiled back.

"You haven't spoken to them, so this warning seems unnecessary."

"Our art gallery is having a private event that requires us to both be there. So, they're laying out the rules for my conduct."

She glanced down again and saw the check there, a check for a lot of money, but she didn't react to it. Her eyes lifted to mine again.

"I don't need the money. I don't want it. Sometimes I think about donating it just to piss them off, but where would that get me?"

She sat there and listened.

"But if I leave the trust, I have no connection to them. We'll never see each other. We'll never cross paths. It'll become so easy to forget I ever existed." I turned to look at the fire, my fingers brushing over my coarse jawline. "I know there will never be a reconciliation. I know it's hopeless. But…I still hope."

Scarlett remained quiet, listening as she stared at the side of my face.

I turned to look at her again. "Will you come with me?"

"Of course."

"It's Saturday night."

"We'll get a pizza afterward and down a bottle of scotch."

I smirked. "I'd like to see you drink scotch."

"I don't love it, but I don't mind it."

"That's sexy." I watched her beautiful face in the glow of the fire. Winter tried to shatter the glass behind me and snuff out the fire that kept her warm. There was something about the look in her eyes, the sadness that swirled like a storm, the slight smile still on her lips, one that was faked just for my benefit. Everything about her captivated me.

She left the armchair and sauntered toward me, but instead of dropping that beautiful ass in my lap, she lowered herself to her knees on the rug in front of me, her hands starting at my thighs and sliding to my knees. "You're sexy." Her hands slid back up my legs and moved to the top of my jeans underneath my shirt. With her eyes locked on mine, she popped the button then pulled down the zipper, getting the snug jeans loose so she could tug them down just enough to give her access to what she needed. She grabbed my dick like a lollipop she'd won at a carnival and pressed her tongue to the base before she slowly rose up, dragging her tongue along my thick vein, and then sealed my head inside her plump lips.

I relaxed in the armchair as my hand dug into her hair, watching her go to town on my big dick. She started off slow, just tasting me and licking me, but then she flattened her tongue and pushed the whole thing to the back of her throat, gagging slightly because it was almost too much for her. She quickly recovered and kept going. "There you go, Pretty…"

21

SCARLETT

After I put on my dress, I clasped the bracelet to my wrist and put the diamond earrings in my lobes. Tonight, I'd chosen to wear a black cocktail dress because black was always the safest bet. My jewelry matched my wedding ring, platinum and shiny. I wondered if his parents would notice me and realize I was married to their son.

Axel grabbed the jacket hanging on the back of the armchair and slipped it on before he secured the button. He could do his own tie without even looking in the mirror because growing up as a wealthy socialite had given him all those skills.

I walked out in my dress and heels, my coat over my arm.

He looked me up and down as he folded down his collar and smoothed out his jacket. He didn't say anything, but his eyes showed his approval. Then a flirty smile moved over his lips as he stepped toward me. "Here." He grabbed my coat and opened it for me, helping me get it on without messing up my hair. "Ready?"

"Yeah."

He opened the door and let me walk out first.

We headed down the hallway, down the stairs, and then entered the elevator.

"You didn't say anything about my dress."

He smirked. "I'll show you how much I like it later." The doors opened, and he blocked them from closing until I stepped out first. He helped me into the car before he left the garage and drove through the busy streets to get to the art gallery. Like always, his hand held mine on my knee, a routine we had established and hadn't broken. When we came to a stoplight, he relaxed in his seat, his elbow propped on the windowsill beside him. He traced the scruff of his beard, staring ahead with a dazed look in his eyes.

"Are you nervous?"

"I don't get nervous."

"You said you didn't do dates either, but now you're married."

That sexy smirk returned. "You're special, baby."

"Why?" I turned to look at him.

His eyes were still on the road, waiting for the light to turn green. "Because you are." The light changed, and he grabbed the wheel so he could drive through the intersection and continue on our way.

The rest of the drive was spent in silence. We pulled up to the art gallery moments later, and the valet took the car before we walked inside. The room was full of people dressed for the occasion, and I wondered if this was all socialites ever did—pick out a new dress and wait for the next party invitation.

Axel slid his arm around my waist and kept it there, introducing me to people he knew from his work in the community or people he'd known his whole life through social circles. If anyone knew that he was estranged from his parents, they didn't seem to show it. And if they believed he was truly guilty of the crimes he'd served two years in prison for, they didn't seem to show that either.

Axel returned from the bar and handed me the glass of wine.

"This is weird."

He took a drink from his glass as his arm returned to my waist, his eyes questioning me.

"Any time we were at the same party in the past, we always had to ignore each other. Now, you introduce me as your wife."

"I'd prefer to introduce you as something else, but it'd probably be inappropriate." He smirked.

I gave him a playful punch in the arm. "Such as?"

His hand moved down and squeezed my ass right there in the middle of the party. "My hot piece of ass."

I gave him another playful smack as I rolled my eyes.

He tugged me close, bringing my lips to his so he could kiss me. And it wasn't a quick kiss on the lips, but a full-on embrace as his hand gripped my ass again. "Don't act like you don't like it, baby."

"I like it, just not in public."

That arrogant grin was on his face. "Yes, you do. I can take you to the ancient Egypt room and fuck you on a sarcophagus. I bet you'd like that." His arm continued to keep me close, close enough that his lips were practically against my cheek.

"You've had too much to drink tonight."

"Drunk or sober, I'm obsessed with you, Pretty." He pulled away and took another sip of his wine, his eyes scanning the room.

I had no idea what his parents looked like, so if they were right next to us, I would have no idea. I wondered if Axel had seen them, but I didn't want to ask if he had and bring down his mood.

"Alexander?" A man called to us from across the room, a man several decades older than Axel, his gray hair starting to turn white in places. He held up his glass then motioned for us to walk over and join him as he spoke to another couple.

Axel took another drink of his wine, downing the entire thing in a single gulp. "Let's do this." He took my hand and guided me over.

I didn't need an introduction to understand exactly what was happening.

The older couple the prime minister spoke to were both pale as ghosts, and that was an odd look in a room that was several degrees too warm. The man put his arm around his wife, and they took a noticeable step back.

"I just wanted to congratulate all of you on the hard work you've done," the prime minister said. "Preserving your history, but also keeping these historic sites available to the public. Most people would have sold everything off or let it fall into ruin, but you have maintained your legacy and the legacy of your people..." He continued on, oblivious to the hostility between the two parties.

I stared at his parents, who both stared at Axel like he was carrying a bloody hatchet. Then in the middle of the prime minister's speech, they turned away and walked off, choosing to be rude instead of suffering their son's presence.

"Uh, did I miss something?" Prime Minister Amato asked, looking at Axel again.

"My parents and I aren't close," Axel said. "We're like the North Pole and Antarctica."

"Oh." He slid his hand into his pocket. "I'm sorry to hear that."

"It is what it is," Axel said. "So, how are the kids?" He brushed it off like it was no big deal, like it didn't make him lose sleep or sulk in the dark alone for several hours at a time.

"Oh, they're great. Janine just started secondary school…" The prime minister brushed off the awkwardness and shared his life with Axel.

I didn't listen. Instead, my eyes followed his parents, seeing them move to another spot in the room. They spoke quietly to each other, their faces still pale, as if being that close to their son was somehow an insult. They looked older than their age, like life had caused them unnecessary stress and advanced aging.

Seeing them avoid Axel like the plague pissed me off to no end. With Axel and the prime minister locked in deep conversation, I stepped away to give them a piece of my mind.

Axel was quick to grab me by the wrist and bring me back—as if he knew exactly where I was going.

I looked at him, my eyes furious.

He stared back, saying nothing as the prime minister continued to carry on.

I tugged on my arm to get free.

His grip tightened. "Let it go." He said it quietly.

The prime minister stopped talking when he picked up on the tension.

"They gave you a restraining order, *not me*." I twisted out of his grasp, so he was forced to release me to avoid breaking my wrist. Then I headed across the room and didn't look back. I moved through the crowd of people and walked right up to them, both of them still locked in a heated conversation. My heart raced like I had sprinted across the room rather than walked. "My name is Scarlett. It's lovely to meet you both." I didn't extend my hand to shake theirs, suspecting they would ignore the gesture.

They both turned to me with quizzical expressions, as if they didn't recognize me from two minutes ago because they'd been too busy looking at Axel.

"I'm married to your son."

The woman looked to her husband, unsure what to do.

He continued to hold a glass of champagne in his hand, but it trembled with nervousness. "I see."

"I wish I could have met you at the wedding, but you didn't come." It made no difference to me that they weren't interested in being my in-laws. My mother wasn't interested in me either, and I didn't lose any sleep over it. But it ripped my husband into a million pieces. "I know how much that hurt Alexander." It was strange to call him by his given name, but that seemed to be how everyone else knew him.

His father continued to stare at me, waiting for me to speak or leave.

"I know he's innocent," I said. "I just wish you knew that too."

He continued to say nothing, like he hoped I would just walk away if he ignored me.

"Ever since the moment I met him, he's been nothing but good to me. I'd given up on men until he came along. Maybe his choice of career is questionable, but you should be proud of who he is as a person—and he's a great man. Life is too short to be estranged from your only son."

It was clear they wouldn't remark on anything I said. They took an oath of silence and stared.

"He cares about both of you—deeply."

Nothing.

"And I know you must care about him." My eyes shifted back and forth between them, pleading with them to have some sanity.

His father dropped his hand from his wife's side. "We gave Alexander everything. All of our resources, all of our time, and all of our love. Even if what you say is true, that he's somehow innocent of a crime for which he was found guilty, he still chose to live a life of criminality—"

"Because you tried so desperately to cut him out of the trust."

"He could have gotten an honorable job—"

"And made a fraction of the salary he's used to. You forced him into this life."

"We are not responsible for Alexander's decision to push drugs on the street," his father said. "And to blame us is immature on your part. His association nearly got me killed, and my arm will never be the same since he chose to rub elbows with the rats in the sewers. An estrangement is the only protection I have against another encounter."

"If he left the business, would you be willing to make amends—"

"No," he snapped. "There are some things you can't take back."

"He didn't intend for you to get hurt—"

"Doesn't matter." Now his voice rose in the middle of the party, the music barely able to drown him out. "I'm ashamed that he's my son. I want nothing to do with him. Our lives would have been better if he'd never been born."

I flinched at those words as if my own father had said them to me. They were so raw and painful, I didn't know how to digest such a horrible, unspeakable statement. "You should be ashamed."

"Alexander is the only thing I'm ashamed of." His arm moved to his wife. "Let's go."

She hadn't said anything the entire time, and her face was scrunched up like all the muscles were working to suppress the tears. But she obeyed and walked off with her husband.

I watched them cross to the other side of the room in an attempt to put distance between us, like I might change my mind and pursue them again. It was tempting, to walk over there and throw a drink in that man's face.

The guests filed out and the music died. Dirty plates were left on the tables, along with empty glasses with puddles of booze left at the bottom. The chandeliers were turned up, dispelling the elegant atmosphere and making it look like a football field under bright lights.

Axel was sitting at one of the abandoned tables, his fingers cupped around an empty glass. His tie had already been tugged loose. He was slouched in the chair, eyes on the glass like his mind was somewhere else.

I sat in the chair beside him. "Want another?"

His eyes lifted to look at me. "Bar's closed."

"I can whip up something."

A slight smirk moved over his lips, but it wasn't genuine. "Surprise me."

I helped myself to the bar, making two old-fashioneds with the orange slice stuck on the rim of the glass, and then returned to my seat beside him.

He grabbed the glass and took a drink, savoring the taste on his tongue. Then he gave a nod in approval. "I'm impressed."

"I used to be a bartender way back when." I took a drink and ignored the burn as it scorched my throat.

"The tips you must have gotten…" He smirked again before he took a drink. "But it was probably nothing compared to the phone numbers."

I grabbed the orange and squeezed it into my glass before I took a drink, noting the refreshing taste of citrus.

He took a big drink then licked his lips.

I waited for him to ask me about the conversation I'd had with his parents, but he never did. "This is a nice building."

"It's as old as the Duomo. My family has renovated it a couple times to keep it standing." He took another drink then left the empty glass on the table, the workers cleaning up around us. "Want me to show you around?"

"Do you actually want to show me around, or just fuck me on a sarcophagus?"

He smirked as he got to his feet. "Let's find out." He took my hand, and we walked down the hallway, heading to the first exhibit, which was everything related to the Renaissance. There were paintings, sculptures, schematics of architecture.

"This place is huge."

"But nothing compared to the Louvre."

"How does someone run a museum? How do you get people to hand over pieces for exhibitions?"

"The museum is considered to be a heritage site. And since it's been designated as such for so long, it's just always been that way." With my hand in his, he guided me down the hallways and into the Byzantine Empire and then the Egyptian section.

"Have you been to Egypt?"

"My family and I went when I was younger. Explored the pyramids."

"Wow, that's so cool."

"It's a lot of stone and sand, if you ask me. Now the beach, that's where it's at."

"Because of the women?" I teased.

"I was a teenager at the time," he said with a grin. "I had different priorities."

We stopped in front of a sphinx statue, protected behind thick glass with several paragraphs of information written beneath it. It was quiet on this side of the building, the sounds of plates and cleaning absent this far from the lobby.

He continued to stare at the sphinx with a haze over his eyes, like he'd had too much to drink or didn't care about the history right in front of his eyes. "My parents always wanted me to be an ambassador…since I was good with people. But I've never been interested in politics. It's just a bunch of bullshit, and you can't punch someone to get something done."

"You are good with people."

"I just know how to smile at the right times." He turned away from the sphinx and looked at me. "So, what did you think of Mom and Dad? They're lovely, aren't they?" His eyes were hazier than they'd ever been, a little watery, and I knew he really did drink too much tonight.

It was the first time I'd ever seen him hit the bottle too hard. There was always a drink in his hand, so I assumed his tolerance was sky-high—but he seemed to have reached his limit this evening. "I'm not their biggest fan."

He gave an exaggerated nod, like that gave him all the details of the conversation. He looked at the sphinx again.

"I'm sorry."

"It's fine." His voice was quiet, so quiet it was practically a whisper. "I didn't expect that conversation to accomplish anything. But at least they met you, I guess."

"It's not my place to say anything, and I should probably keep my mouth shut—"

"I never want you to keep your mouth shut, baby." He turned to me, looking at me with hooded eyes. "You're smart. Beautiful. Passionate. I hang on to every damn word that leaves those lips."

Now I knew what kind of drunk he was—a sweet one. "Your dad's a prick."

He smiled then released a chuckle. "Yep. That's my old man."

"I asked if he'd be willing to reconcile if you left this profession, but his answer was no."

"Told you. He wants nothing to do with me."

But I hadn't believed it until I'd seen it with my own eyes. "I'm sorry."

"Not your fault, baby."

"I went over there to make things better, but all I did was make myself angry."

"Welcome to my life." He grabbed his tie and tugged it farther apart like it was constricting his neck. "But it doesn't matter." He swayed slightly, but his strong body righted itself instantly. "You're my family, baby." His hand dug into my hair, and he cupped my face, bringing me close to him. "This is what matters."

My heart burst from my chest with both joy…and utter pain.

His hand went to my stomach, and he cupped it, even though there was nothing there. "We'll have our own babies, and I'll be the best father there ever was. My love will be unconditional, and they'll never wonder if

I'll be there for them. They'll know there's nothing they could ever do to lose me."

"Axel…"

He rested his head against mine, his big arms pulling me close, his hand supporting the back of my neck.

My face was against his chest, and the guilt pounded over me in waves. The conversations I'd had with my father passed across my mind, intensifying the guilt.

"We're a family," he said as he held me. "You're my family."

The asphalt was wet because it had rained the night before.

When I stepped out of the car, I felt the tip of my heel slip slightly because of the slickness. The cold air hit me instantly, and I felt it shrink my lungs when I took a breath. I walked to the double doors and let myself inside, the warmth hugging me and making me forget the winter misery.

I checked in with my father's butler and let him know I'd arrived before I took a seat in the parlor, looking outside at the darkness. It wasn't even seven o'clock in the evening, but it looked like midnight. I stared until my father joined me, wearing dark jeans and a brown jacket.

"Hello, sweetheart." He leaned down to give me a hug and kissed me on the temple. "It's been a long winter, hasn't it?" He moved to the chair across from me, and his butler immediately brought our refreshments and appetizers.

"The longest of my life." It was always raining. It was always overcast. It was always cold. But it was definitely better than other years, because I had a sexy man in my bed to keep me warm.

My father took a drink of his wine. "I'm always happy to see you, but what brings you by?"

I hadn't told him I was coming. My thoughts had become too heavy for me to carry any longer. I'd lied to Axel and told him I'd already made dinner plans with my father, and he didn't question it. "I just haven't seen you in a while."

He gave a slight nod, but his intelligent eyes showed he didn't believe me. "Nothing too interesting has happened in my life since we last spoke. I went to the opera the other night, and then I tried that new restaurant they finally opened."

"Who did you go to the opera with?"

"A friend," he said quickly and didn't elaborate. "How are you?"

"I met Axel's parents the other night. They're assholes. Well, his father is. His mother didn't say a word."

My father drank his wine.

"I just don't understand how a father can turn his back on his own son."

He remained quiet, bringing his hands together between his knees. "Families can be complicated."

"But they shouldn't be complicated." Axel never described the depth of his pain, but I could see it written clearly across his face, could see it in the way his eyes fell. "It makes me appreciate what we have, because I never have to worry where we stand."

He lifted his eyes to look at me, warmth in his gaze. "There's nothing you could do to make me love you less."

"I know." And that meant the world to me. I had a place to go, a place where I belonged—always. "So I know you'll understand what I'm about to tell you." The guilt was too much for me to bear. My shoulders sagged under the weight. My heart was about to burst from the pressure. "I know our plan is to cut Axel out and reclaim the business, but I don't think I can do that."

His warmth slowly hardened into icicles. His eyes flicked back and forth between mine, his mind searching for a contradiction in my words.

"I can't betray him."

He remained motionless, his breathing slow, his eyes becoming callous once he accepted what I said. "Don't let him manipulate you, sweetheart."

"He's not manipulating me—"

"He's not stupid. Wooing you is his way of preventing a retaliation."

"There would be no need for a retaliation if you hadn't screwed him over."

He was silent, but he drew in a deep and heavy breath.

"Look…" I didn't want to fight. I didn't want to disappoint him. "He's a good man—"

"He *cheated* on you, Scarlett," he snapped. "You're very quick to forget."

"I don't want to live in the past anymore. That moment is not a reflection of our current relationship. He's offered to split his share with me. We've gotten what we wanted. We have the business."

"It's not our business if we have to share it."

"Even if we got it back, we would lose all those partnerships and would be back to what we were making before—"

"Doesn't matter."

"And even if we succeed, Axel and Theo will just retaliate. It'll never end—"

"If Axel really cares for you, he won't do a damn thing."

"I just mean…" I steadied my voice because when I yelled, he yelled. "It's going to go back and forth… indefinitely. Let's appreciate what we have and move on."

My father abruptly rose from the chair and started to pace, arms crossed over his chest. He walked to the window and looked outside, looked through the streaming raindrops to the dark terrace outside.

"I can't betray him. I'm sorry." I couldn't lie to Axel. I couldn't bed him at night then plot against him in the morning. I couldn't turn my back on him when there was this…connection between us. It was always there, no matter what we went through—unconditional.

My father was quiet for a long time.

I stared at my glass of wine and waited for him to speak. The tension was suffocating. His back remained turned to me as he shut me out of his thoughts. "I ask that you drop this."

He gave a heavy sigh.

I knew my words would anger him, but I said them anyway. "I care for him." I cared for him deeply…madly.

My father never spoke.

"Please don't be mad at me—"

"I'm not angry." He turned back to me, his hands moving into his pockets, his stare cold but his voice normal. "Just disappointed." He slowly walked over to me. "I raised you to be smarter than this, wiser than this." He dropped back into the chair across from me. "A day will come when he'll betray you again—and you'll know that I was right. But for now...I accept your decision." He grabbed the bottle of wine and refilled his glass, pouring far too much. Then he took a drink, his throat shifting as he downed it like water. When he returned the glass to the table, his movements were so sloppy he almost knocked the bottle over.

I didn't want to end the conversation like this, not when I felt his seething anger like flames from a fireplace. "How are things with the Colombians?"

He grabbed his glass again and took another drink, drinking more in a single sitting than I'd ever seen before. He set the empty glass on the coffee table between us. "I have a meeting with them in—" he pushed back the sleeve of his jacket to look at his watch "—in twenty minutes."

"They're here?"

"Yes." It took him a while to make eye contact with me, like he dreaded the moment our stares realigned. "Axel told me he wouldn't accept their initial proposal, so I need to negotiate. Your husband and I don't see eye to eye on this issue."

"What was his counter?"

"Two and a half percent and their initial fee."

"That's a lot less than ten percent."

"They want to be considered a partner, and since it's their product we're selling, I think it's reasonable. I'm not one to pay more than I have to, but I think it's worth keeping the peace. The Colombians do things differently."

"Where are you meeting them?"

"At the facility."

"Should I tag along?" I asked. "I've always been good at negotiating."

"Not a bad idea," he said. "Men are usually on their best behavior when there's a woman in the room." He grabbed the bottle to pour another glass.

"Dad." I steadied his hand and gently redirected him to the table. "You've had two glasses of wine in five minutes. Let's take a break."

His fingers continued to grip the neck of the bottle, and for a moment, it seemed like he wouldn't let go. But after a breath, he finally relaxed his fingers and released the bottle. "I apologize, sweetheart. Wine has always been my weakness." He straightened and flashed me a smile, the kind that didn't reach his eyes. "We should get going if we don't want to be late."

The production facility looked abandoned from the outside, because if it was in full operation in the middle of the night, it would raise some eyebrows and draw attention from the wrong people. But once you walked through the door, the warmth from the heaters struck you and the lights made you squint.

We headed downstairs to where the lab was situated, and the lab technicians and chemists were there working, making batches around the clock just to meet our quota for the week.

We moved farther down the hallway into a private room and took a seat. Old carpet was on the floor, and the table was one of those cheap ones stocked in break rooms. The counter held a microwave and an old coffeemaker.

My father took a seat and automatically lifted his sleeve to check the time. Then he pulled out his phone and started texting or typing emails.

I could still feel the tension between us. My father was distant with his silence. He had a bit of that same haze Axel had had over the weekend, like he'd had too much to drink but his mind continued to fight it.

It was cold in the back room, so I cinched the tie of my coat to keep it tight around my body.

Minutes passed, and then voices were audible, uproarious laughter and booming tones, like they were about to head to a party rather than an important meeting. Their footsteps grew louder, and then the guys entered, wearing long-sleeved shirts and hoodies, some of them with tattoos on their faces.

My father rose to his feet and shook hands with them. "Nice to see you, gentlemen." When the guys all turned to look at me, my father made the introduction. "This is my daughter, Scarlett. She helps with the business. She's going to sit in, if that's okay."

One of the guys sat across from me, grinning wide. "Oh, that's more than fine." A couple of his teeth were missing, and there was a gold shine from the deeper part of his mouth.

The other guys took a seat, one with a ponytail.

A long stretch of silence ensued.

They all stared at me.

My father cleared his throat. "I'll cut straight to the chase." He crossed his leg and rested his ankle on the opposite knee. "Ten percent is too high. Our counter is two and a half percent, in addition to your current compensation."

None of the guys moved or reacted, as if they didn't understand what my father said or had expected him to say those exact words.

The one who'd smiled at me finally gave a nod. "Two and a half percent…seems a little insulting."

"That's a lot of money, Christian," my father said. "A lot."

"But ten percent is *a lot* more money," Christian said. "Money we deserve."

My father stared at him, looking perfectly calm despite the rising tensions.

"You know, I was actually doing you a favor," Christian said. "There's nothing stopping us from selling our product directly to the European countries.

Truth be told, we don't even need you. So, if you aren't going to pay us, then we'll pay ourselves."

"It's a lot more complicated than you realize," my father said. "We have the connections to deal with the regulations and border transport. That's not something you'll be able to replicate—"

"It is if I take the business from you."

Now the air in the room changed, going from warm to scalding hot like a pot of boiling water on the stove. I felt my breathing deepen, felt my heart pick up in speed, but I kept up my poker face. My eyes shifted from my father.

"Take it from me?" my father asked, smirking.

"Someone else did, right?" Christian cocked his head. "So what's to stop me from taking it from all of you?"

"No one took it from me," my father said calmly. "I partnered with a powerful man, and that's why we've expanded our distribution—"

"You're going to lie to me?" Christian snapped. "You're going to look right into my face and lie?"

A period of silence passed, feeling like an eternity. I couldn't keep my breathing steady, not when I felt the danger like it was pressed right against the back of my neck. We had armed men on the property, but they were in the other room watching the chemists make the product.

"I don't think we want to do business with a liar," Christian said. "Not my preference."

My pulse was so strong in my neck, I actually felt the vein twitch. As discreetly as I could, I reached for my phone in my pocket, and without thinking the plan through, I dropped my location to Axel then silenced my phone. If he called, it might draw attention to me, and I had no idea what these guys might do. If Axel called and I didn't answer, he would assume something was wrong and come as quick as he could. I returned the phone to my pocket and watched the scene unfold.

"So, we can do this one of two ways," Christian said. "You can yield and give me what I need to continue operations. Or we can do things the other way…"

How my father remained calm was a fucking mystery. "Or there's option three."

"I don't think there's an option three, Dante."

"I'll give you fifteen percent, and we forget this whole thing."

Christian turned to his guys and laughed, loudly and obnoxiously. "You're funny, Dante."

"Fifteen percent is generous."

"Come on, Dante," Christian said. "We both know there's no going back now. After I agree, you'll just have me killed. So now, I have to kill you." He gave a shrug. "I told you I was doing you a favor."

My father took a long pause. "Even if I wanted to yield, I have two partners."

"And you'll tell me everything I need to know, and I'll eliminate them," Christian said. "Problem solved. So tell me what I want to know, and I'll make it quick. I've never been into the whole pain and suffering thing."

I should speak up and try to resolve this, but I was so fucking scared and out of my element here.

My father was quiet for a long time. "If you aren't into pain and suffering, you'll excuse my daughter from the room. No reason for her to be involved in this."

"You involved her when you brought her here, Dante."

"Let her go," he said calmly. "Please."

Christian shifted his gaze to me. "Wish I could, but she's important to the next part of our plan. Bringing her is actually a huge help for us. Saved us a lot of time." He looked at my father again. "We know she's married to your partner, so she's the key to ensuring his cooperation."

We'd walked right into a trap—and I wasn't walking out of it.

The guy in the ponytail left his chair and walked around the table toward me.

"What are you doing?" My father's voice turned frantic, and he got out of his chair.

I was out of my chair too, dragging the chair in front of me as an obstacle between us. "Don't fucking touch me."

He smiled, and he was missing most of his teeth too.

My father stepped in front of me. "Christian, I'll cooperate. Just leave my daughter alone."

I hoped Axel saw my location. I hoped he wasn't in the gym or in the shower, having no idea that we both needed help.

"They aren't mutually exclusive, Dante," Christian said from his chair.

My father continued to block me from the assailants. "Guards!"

"No one's coming," Christian said. "My guys came in behind us and killed them all with syringes."

The guy rushed my father.

My father threw a punch and then ducked the attack. Blows went back and forth, and I was surprised my father could hold his own against a guy at least a decade younger. "Scarlett, run!"

There was nowhere to go, not when the other three guys were near the door.

Christian beckoned me forward with his fingertips. "Come here, sweetheart."

I was so sick. So fucking sick.

I grabbed the chair that had been pushed aside and slammed it into the guy who'd just punched my father in the face.

The man collapsed to the floor and gave a loud moan.

The other three guys jumped to their feet as my father went on to the next one.

I dropped down and searched the guy for a weapon. Their guns had been stripped at the entrance, but maybe he had a knife or something.

I heard my father grunt when he was punched in the stomach, and my hands shook as I explored the guy's pockets. I finally found a pocketknife, the kind used to open mail or other household packages. It wasn't much of a weapon, but I could make it into a damn weapon.

I got to my feet, seeing one of the men punch my father so hard he crashed to the floor. Just then, another guy came around the table and threw himself at me. My hand automatically shot up and dug the blade deep into his neck, hitting him in the artery. I knew I'd hit my mark when the blood started to squirt. "Oh fuck."

"Get in here!" Christian yelled down the hallway.

My father was collapsed on the floor, knocked out cold.

Christian and his last guy came at me from either side of the table, blocking my exit on both sides.

I kicked the chair at one of them then threw myself across the table, sliding until I hit the floor on the other side. I forced myself up and lunged at the door, but I stopped when I saw the guys running down the hallway.

Then I was grabbed by the throat, a heavy arm squeezing me so tight, he nearly broke my neck. I couldn't breathe, only flailed my arms around as I tried to get free.

"This bitch is feisty." It was Christian who had me. "We'll have some fun with her before we give her back."

"Let her go." My father's voice came from behind me.

"Knock that fucker out."

A burst of rage surged through me, and I slammed my head back as hard as I could, hitting Christian square in the nose.

"Fuck." He dropped me and reached for his face.

I threw myself at him and knocked him to the floor.

My father went for the other guy, blood stained all over his face.

Christian pulled me down and punched me in the face, then punched me again, making blood pour from my mouth and nose. "Still sit, bitch."

I scratched his face, digging my nails as deep as I could go.

Then he grabbed my throat again and squeezed. "Fuck it, I'm killing her." He squeezed me tight, refusing to let any air reach my lungs. Seconds passed, and I couldn't fight it. Reality started to slip away.

Gunshots were audible in the distance. Then I heard yells and screams. I lay there, my vision blurry, the pain suddenly gone because I couldn't feel anything at all.

I was aware of the pressure leaving my neck and the air that finally flooded into my lungs. Christian was yanked off me and slammed into the wall. A gunshot went off, and he was dead. Another went off, and then it went quiet.

"Baby."

I inhaled a deep breath when I heard that voice. "Babe?" I released a series of coughs, the air hurting my lungs when I tried to speak.

He lifted me from the floor and cradled me in his arms. Livid eyes roamed over my appearance, checking my face and the blood that dripped to my chin. "Jesus Christ."

"Scarlett." My father's voice came closer. "Sweetheart, are you—"

"*Fuck off, asshole.*" Axel placed me in a chair. He supported me as I continued to cough.

"It was a trap," my father said. "An ambush."

Axel left me and rushed my father, punching him so hard in the face, he hit the wall then slid to the floor. "Why the fuck is she here? Why the fuck would you bring *my wife* anywhere near these scumbags?"

"Axel, stop," I said between my breaths.

"What the fuck is wrong with you?" Axel kicked my father and made him groan. "You don't give a shit about her and never have."

"Please stop," I said. "Axel, stop."

Then Axel spat on him, spat right on his face.

He came back to me, cradling my face in his hands. "Are you alright?"

"I'm fine."

"I can take you to the hospital."

I shook my head. "I'm just shaken up, is all."

One of the guys handed Axel a tissue, and he proceeded to wipe the blood off my face.

I knew I was safe, but I was still overwhelmed by everything that had just gone down and the horrible fear of what could have happened if Axel hadn't come.

"Baby, I'm here." He bunched up the bloody tissue and tossed it on the floor. "You're safe now."

"I know." I continued to breathe hard, like the danger was still in the room. "It all happened so fast…"

He brought me in close and squeezed me tight, pressing a kiss to my temple. "Baby, I love you." He squeezed me hard and inhaled a deep breath, like he needed the hug more than I did.

My cheek rested against his shoulder, and I let myself be cocooned by his hold. It took me a second to realize what he'd said…and how he'd said it so effortlessly. The adrenaline paused when I let his words sink into my soul.

"Scarlett." My father drew near, his face bloody and swollen from the beating he'd taken.

Axel released me with a heavy breath that made his nostrils flare. He stepped aside, but not before giving my father the look of death.

"Sweetheart." My father took a knee and hugged me. "I'm so sorry."

"It's okay. You're okay?"

"I'm fine." He squeezed me like I was a little girl. "I'm just glad you're alright." He pulled away to look at me, tears in his eyes as he cupped my face, the emotion so potent that those tears turned into rivers and streaked down his face. "I shouldn't have brought you here—"

"Damn fucking right." Axel grabbed a chair and threw it against the wall.

The sound made us both jerk.

"But you have to parade her around like a fucking trophy!" he yelled. "Because you're a sick fuck."

When my father looked at Axel, the emotional tears were still in his eyes, but he looked livid at the same time. "None of this would have happened if you'd just given them the ten percent—"

"No, they would have killed you, and my wife would be safe in my bed right now. That's what should have happened, and I wish it had." He grabbed the chair and threw it at the wall again, as if he was trying to break it down.

"Axel," I said, trying to subdue his anger.

"I hate this motherfucker with every fiber of my being." He grabbed my father by the arm and shoved him into the wall. "Has been ruining my life since the day I met him."

"Stop it." I grabbed Axel by the arm and tugged him back. "I mean it."

My father leaned against the wall as he panted, staring Axel down as a mortal enemy.

I continued to grip his arm. "My father would never knowingly put me in danger. Let it go."

"Let it go." Axel turned to look down at me. "Oh baby, if only you knew how much shit I let go." He turned and slammed his fist into the table, hitting it so hard a dent formed in the steel surface. "If you ever pull this shit again, I'll kill you. I will slam your body into the floor as many times as it takes to break it." Axel got in my father's face. "You fucking understand me?"

My father remained against the wall, staring Axel down with equal hatred.

Axel grabbed him by the neck and slammed him into the wall. "I didn't hear you."

"Axel, I told you to stop," I said.

"She's mine now," Axel said. "My wife. My family. My responsibility. You understand me?"

Before he could be slammed into the wall again, my father said, "Yes…I understand you."

Axel finally released him before he looked at me again. "I'll wait for you outside." He walked down the hallway, his guys following him, leaving my father and me alone together with the dead bodies.

My father remained against the wall, blood stains all over the collar of his jacket. He stared at the floor for a while, one foot planted against the wall.

Everything flashed across my eyes repeatedly, from beginning to end, in a nanosecond. I would have nightmares for a long time. Not even Axel could keep them away.

My father left the wall and pulled up a chair across from me. He sat down, releasing a heavy breath since it'd been a long and exhausting night. "There are no words to convey how fucking sorry I am." His head was bowed in shame, eyes on the floor between us.

I stilled, hearing my father curse for one of the first times.

"Axel is right. Don't be angry with him."

"I'm not angry with him…or with you."

He lifted his chin and looked at me.

"We're okay. That's all that matters."

"I didn't anticipate the events to unfold like that."

"I know, it's okay."

"It's not okay," he whispered. "It's not…"

My hand reached for his and held it.

He stared at our joined hands and gave it a squeeze. "You're too good to me, sweetheart."

"Not as good as you are to me."

He didn't lift his head. Didn't smile. Just sat there and held my hand.

When we walked out, Axel was leaning against the door of the SUV, arms crossed over his chest, his jaw tight with suppressed rage. His eyes immediately locked on mine and followed me as I walked with my father to his car. We hugged each other goodbye before he got into his car and drove away.

I walked back to the SUV, watching Axel stare me down like I was the one who'd done something wrong.

He stared at me for another moment before he righted himself and opened the door for me.

I got into the seat and buckled my safety belt. The engine came to life a moment later, and the heater kicked on.

Axel got into the other seat beside me, and the driver took us home.

We spent the drive in silence, but his unsaid words filled the car. He was livid, and no amount of silence could dwarf that truth.

After we were dropped off, we made the long journey from the elevator to the stairs and then to the bedroom. The second the door shut, he snapped. "Let's get something straight here." He walked up to me, in my face, not moved by the bruising around my mouth and nose. "Don't you ever put yourself in that position again. I don't know if he asked you or you asked him—*and I don't want to know*. Either answer is just going to piss me off. I want your word that you'll stick to bookkeeping and that's it."

I'd wanted this business for a long time. Wanted to be the one in charge, to have a yacht like my father, to be a rich woman driving through the streets in one of my many cars. But tonight showed me how useless I really was. It showed me how dark the underworld could truly be. "I promise."

Axel breathed hard in front of me, his chest rising and falling with his heavy breaths. He clearly expected opposition or an argument, and he didn't know how to accept my surrender. He continued to breathe as his eyes shifted back and forth between mine.

"I'm not cut out for this kind of life…" My voice trailed off, growing defeated. "I'm not sure why I ever thought otherwise."

Slowly, his anger faded, the tint in his face paling.

"In fact…I'm not sure I want to be involved at all anymore." The game never ended. Axel teamed up with Theo and tricked my father, and then our suppliers made idiots out of us both. You always had to stay one step ahead, and if you failed, it would cost you your life.

He gave a curt nod in acceptance.

I stepped away. "I'm going to take a shower."

He let me go, but his eyes drilled into my back. "So you're going to act like you didn't hear me?"

I stilled, facing our bedroom, feeling his hot stare in the back of my head.

"Just pretend it never happened?" His voice was like venom from a sharp pair of fangs.

I slowly turned back around, seeing those blue eyes turn volcanic.

"Because I fucking meant it," he snapped. "And I'll say it again—*I love you*." He breathed hard again, his jawline sharp as he clenched his jaw. If there was no sound to the scene, it would look like he hated me rather than loved me. "This is where you say it back."

The adrenaline returned, like a storm battling a coast, a siege of a castle. My fingertips were cold to the touch but beaded with sweat. I swallowed air because my mouth was dry. I held his powerful stare but didn't have the words.

"I loved you then, but I was too much of a pussy to say it."

His words were like a wrecking ball against my heart. "So you loved me but left me anyway? You loved me but replaced me with someone else? That makes no sense, Axel." I'd just survived a horrible ordeal, and I would be shaken up for days, if not weeks, but we were fighting like cats and dogs.

He gave an angry sigh. "I loved you then, and I love you now. And all that time in between, I still loved you. I could have lost you tonight, so I'm not going to spend another moment pretending you aren't the love of my life—because you are."

I looked away, his words too intimate for me to accept. They made me feel so warm and alive…but they also ripped me apart. I tried not to live in the past, but everything flashed before my eyes in a heartbeat. "I'm going to shower—"

"No, we're doing this." He crossed the distance between us and got in my face. "We're doing this because it is long overdue. You think I married you to get back at your father?" he asked incredulously. "I married you because I was in love with you. Because I knew it was the only way I could get you back."

I tried to turn away, but he yanked me back.

"Tell me you love me."

I kept my eyes off him. "I'm not…" There were too many words in my head to get out. "I'm not there yet."

"Yes, you are."

"It's hard to hear you say this…because of the way you hurt me."

"Baby—"

"I can't just let it go. I can't just forget about it. It's not that easy. It wasn't even that long ago."

His hand continued to grip my arm. "Look at me."

"No." My eyes stayed on the floor.

"Baby, look at me."

I shook my head.

His voice dropped. "Please."

I closed my eyes, the sound of his voice too beautiful to resist. I took a breath before I lifted my chin and met his gaze.

His eyes shifted back and forth between mine.

"Trust me," he said. "I'd die for you. I'd kill for you. I love you more than any man has ever loved a woman. I'm so fucking in love with you it makes me want to explode. Don't let the past interfere with this moment…because it's real."

My eyes were desperate to flick away, the emotion in his eyes eliciting emotion in mine.

He squeezed my wrist. "It's fucking real." His hand left my wrist and snaked into my hair. "You know it is."

I lowered my gaze to his chin, my hand gripping his wrist. "I—I don't know why I believe you. I don't know what it is. I just do."

"Because you know me, baby."

I found the strength to look at him again.

"You know my heart. You know my soul. You have my fucking back, always have." His fingers dug deeper into my hair. "And I have yours—always. I want you to say it back, but if you can't, it's okay. Because I know you…I know your heart, your soul, all of you. And I know you feel the same way."

Wow, that wasn't easy but we got there...sorta. Is this the calm before the storm? You won't believe what happens next in **_It Ruins Me_**.

Sign up for Penelope's newsletter to hear all her fun stories and stay up to date on new releases. There's also giveaways and access to limited edition hardbacks!

Printed in Great Britain
by Amazon